ANSWERED
PRAYERS

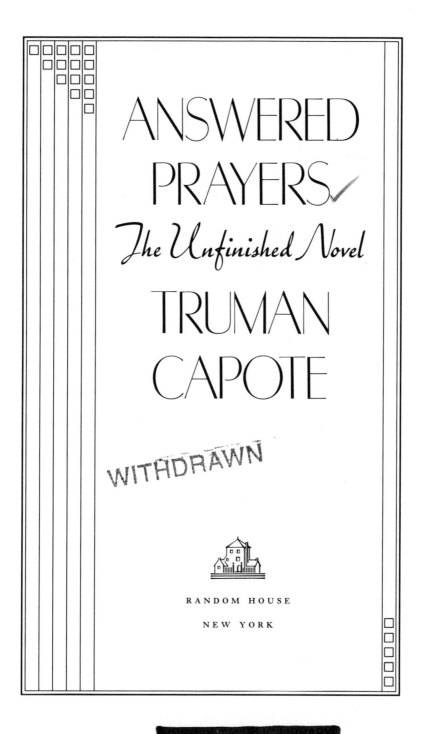

ANSWERED PRAYERS

The Unfinished Novel

TRUMAN CAPOTE

RANDOM HOUSE

NEW YORK

Library of Congress Cataloging in Publication Data
Capote, Truman, 1924–1984
Answered prayers.
I. Title.
PS3505.A59A83 1987   813'.54   86–10110
ISBN 0-394-55645-3

Manufactured in the United States of America
2 4 6 8 9 7 5 3
First Edition

Typography and binding design by J. K. Lambert

"More tears are shed over answered prayers than unanswered ones."

CONTENTS

EDITOR'S NOTE

On January 5, 1966, Truman Capote signed a contract with Random House for a new book to be called *Answered Prayers.* The advance against royalties was $25,000, and the delivery date was January 1, 1968. The novel, Truman maintained, would be a contemporary equivalent of Proust's masterpiece, *Remembrance of Things Past,* and would examine the small world of the very rich —part aristocratic, part café society—of Europe and the east coast of the United States.

1966 was a wonderful year for Truman. Two weeks after he signed the contract for *Answered Prayers, In Cold Blood* was published in book form with enormous fanfare and to general acclaim. During the subsequent week the author's picture appeared on the cover of several national magazines, and his new work was given the lead review in virtually every Sunday book section. In the course of the year, *In Cold Blood* sold more than 300,000 copies and was on *The New York Times* best-seller list for thirty-seven weeks. (Eventually it outsold every other nonfiction book in 1966 save for two self-help books; since then it has been published in some two dozen foreign editions and has sold almost five million copies in the United States alone.)

During this year Truman was everywhere at once, granting interviews by the score, appearing on television talk shows a number of times, vacationing on yachts and in grand country houses, and delighting in his fame and fortune. The culmination of this heady period was his still-remembered "Black and White Ball" given in late November 1966 at the Plaza in honor of Kay Graham, the publisher of the *Washington Post*, a party that received as much coverage in the national press as an East-West summit meeting.

Truman felt he deserved this respite, and most of his friends did too; the research and writing of *In Cold Blood* had taken almost six years, and had been a traumatic experience for him. Nevertheless, despite the distractions, he talked constantly about *Answered Prayers* in this interval. But though he wrote a number of short stories and magazine pieces in the next few years, he did not address himself to the novel; as a result, in May 1969 the original contract was superseded by a three-book agreement changing the delivery date to January 1973 and substantially increasing the advance. In mid-1973 the deadline was advanced to January 1974, and six months later it was changed again to September 1977. (Subse-

quently, in the spring of 1980, one last amendment specified a
delivery date of March 1, 1981, and further raised the advance to
$1 million, to be paid only on delivery of the work.)

Still, Truman published several books in these years, though
the contents of most of them had been written in the 1940's and
1950's. In 1966 Random House issued *A Christmas Memory,* written originally in 1958; in 1968 *The Thanksgiving Visitor,* a short
story published in a magazine in 1967; in 1969 a twentieth-anniver-
sary edition, with a graceful, newly written introduction, of *Other
Voices, Other Rooms,* his first novel which had electrified the literary establishment in 1948; in 1973 a collection called *The Dogs Bark,*
all but three pieces of which had been written many years before.
Only *Music for Chameleons*—which was to be published in 1980,
and which some people, friends as well as critics, felt was not up
to his earlier works—contained new material, both fiction and
nonfiction.

Let Truman speak for himself about this period. In the preface
to *Music for Chameleons* he wrote:

For four years, roughly from 1968 through 1972, I spent most of my
time reading and selecting, rewriting and indexing my own letters,
other people's letters, my diaries and journals (which contain detailed
accounts of hundreds of scenes and conversations) for the years 1943
through 1965. I intended to use much of this material in a book I had
long been planning: a variation on the nonfiction novel. I called the

book *Answered Prayers,* which is a quote from Saint Thérèse,* who said: "More tears are shed over answered prayers than unanswered ones." In 1972 I began work on this book by writing the last chapter first (it's always good to know where one's going). Then I wrote the first chapter, "Unspoiled Monsters." Then the fifth, "A Severe Insult to the Brain." Then the seventh, "La Côte Basque." I went on in this manner, writing different chapters out of sequence. I was able to do this only because the plot—or rather plots—was true, and all the characters were real: it wasn't difficult to keep it all in mind, for I hadn't invented anything.

Finally, over a period of a few months in late 1974 and early 1975, Truman showed me four chapters from *Answered Prayers*—"Mojave,"† "La Côte Basque," "Unspoiled Monsters" and "Kate McCloud"—and announced that he was going to publish them in *Esquire.* I was against this plan, feeling that he was revealing too much of the book too soon, and said so, but Truman, who considered himself a master publicist, was not to be deterred. (If Bennett Cerf, who was also a close friend and confidant of the author, had been alive—he had died in 1971—perhaps our combined disap-

---

*A mistake, probably on the part of Random House; it was actually St. Teresa of Avila.

†Originally "Mojave" was to have been the second chapter of the novel and was ostensibly an attempt by its protagonist, P. B. Jones (a sort of dark Doppelgänger of the author himself), to write a short story. But some years later Truman decided that it didn't belong in the book, and it was published in *Music for Chameleons* as a short story.

proval would have dissuaded Truman, but I doubt it; he felt he knew exactly what he was doing.)

As it turned out, he *didn't* know what he was doing. "Mojave" was the first chapter to appear and caused some talk, but the next, "La Côte Basque," produced an explosion which rocked that small society which Truman had set out to describe. Virtually every friend he had in this world ostracized him for telling thinly disguised tales out of school, and many of them never spoke to him again.

Truman defiantly professed to be undismayed by the furor ("What did they expect?" he was quoted as saying. "I'm a writer, and I use everything. Did all those people think I was there just to entertain them?"), but there is no doubt that he was shaken by the reaction, and I am convinced it was one of the reasons why he apparently stopped working, at least temporarily, on *Answered Prayers* after the publication of "Unspoiled Monsters" and "Kate McCloud" in *Esquire* in 1976.

From 1960, when we first met, to 1977 Truman and I saw each other frequently, both in and out of the office, traveling twice to Kansas together while he was working on *In Cold Blood,* and once spending a week together in Santa Fe. I also visited him during the winters three or four times in Palm Springs, where he had a house for a few years; in addition, by coincidence he owned a house and I rented one in Sagaponack, a small farming community near the sea on eastern Long Island.

Professionally my work for Truman during this period was undemanding. (For example, virtually all of the editorial work on *In Cold Blood* was done by Mr. Shawn and others at *The New Yorker*, where it first appeared in four installments in October and November 1965.) Still, our working relationship was immensely rewarding. I recall with particular pleasure Truman giving me the chapter of "Unspoiled Monsters" to read one afternoon in 1975. I did so overnight, and found it almost flawless save for one small false note. When he called me the next morning for my reaction, I was full of enthusiasm, but did mention my cavil, a word used by Miss Victoria Self in dialogue only half a page after the reader first meets her. "She wouldn't have used that word," I said to Truman; "she would have said ———." (I can't remember my suggested substitute.) Truman laughed with delight. "I reread the chapter last night," he said. "There was only one change I wanted to make, and I was calling now to tell you to change that word to exactly what you just suggested." It was an all-too-rare moment of mutual congratulation in the peculiar relationship between authors and editors. It was not *self*-congratulation; rather, each of us was pleased by the *other*.

I quote again from Truman's preface to *Music for Chameleons*, a few lines farther on:

... I did stop working on *Answered Prayers* in September 1977, a fact that had nothing to do with any public reaction to those parts of the book already published. The halt happened because I was in a helluva lot of trouble: I was suffering a creative crisis and a personal one at the same time. As the latter was unrelated, or very little related, to the former, it is only necessary to remark on the creative chaos.

Now, torment though it was, I'm glad it happened; after all, it altered my entire comprehension of writing, my attitude toward art and life and the balance between the two, and my understanding of the difference between what is true and what is *really* true.

To begin with, I think most writers, even the best, overwrite. I prefer to underwrite. Simple, clear as a country creek. But I felt my writing was becoming too dense, that I was taking three pages to arrive at effects I ought to be able to achieve in a single paragraph. Again and again I read all that I had written on *Answered Prayers,* and I began to have doubts —not about the material or my approach, but about the texture of the writing itself. I reread *In Cold Blood* and had the same reaction: there were too many areas where I was not writing as well as I could, where I was not delivering the total potential. Slowly, but with accelerating alarm, I read every word I'd ever published, and decided that never, not once in my writing life, had I completely exploded all the energy and esthetic excitements that material contained. Even when it was good, I could see that I was never working with more than half, sometimes only a third, of the powers at my command. Why?

The answer, revealed to me after months of meditation, was simple but not very satisfying. Certainly it did nothing to lessen my depression; indeed, it thickened it. For the answer created an apparently unsolvable problem, and if I couldn't solve it, I might as well quit writing. The problem was: how can a writer successfully combine within a single form

—say the short story—all he knows about every other form of writing? For this was why my work was often insufficiently illuminated; the voltage was there, but by restricting myself to the techniques of whatever form I was working in, I was not using everything I knew about writing —all I'd learned from film scripts, plays, reportage, poetry, the short story, novellas, the novel. A writer ought to have all his colors, all his abilities available on the same palette for mingling (and, in suitable instances, simultaneous application). But how?

I returned to *Answered Prayers*. I removed one chapter* and rewrote two others.† An improvement, definitely an improvement. But the truth was, I had to go back to kindergarten. Here I was—off again on one of those grim gambles! But I was excited; I felt an invisible sun shining on me. Still, my first experiments were awkward. I truly felt like a child with a box of crayons.

Unfortunately, some of what Truman writes in the two excerpts quoted above can't be taken at face value. For example, though a thorough search was made of all the author's effects after his death by Alan Schwartz, his lawyer and literary executor, Gerald Clarke, his biographer, and myself, almost none of the letters, diaries or journals he mentions has ever been found.‡ (This

---

*"Mojave."

†Only the *Esquire* versions of the three chapters in this book have been found.

‡What *was* found—enough to fill eight large cartons—was sifted through, page by page, and roughly catalogued by Gerald Clarke and the editor in 1984 and 1985. The material consisted of holograph originals and typed first, second and third drafts of several stories and novels; *The New Yorker* galleys of *In Cold*

is particularly damning, since Truman was a pack rat; he kept virtually everything, and there was no reason to destroy such papers.) Moreover, there was no evidence of "A Severe Insult to the Brain" or of that last chapter which he claimed in his preface to have written first. (It was to be called "Father Flanagan's All-Night Nigger-Queen Kosher Café"; other chapters that he mentioned in conversations with me and others from time to time were "Yachts and Things" and "And Audrey Wilder Sang," a chapter about Hollywood.)

After 1976, Truman's and my relationship slowly deteriorated. My hunch is that it began when he realized that I had been right about publishing the installments in *Esquire,* though of course I never taxed him about this. He may also have realized that his writing powers were waning, and feared that I would be too stern a judge. Further, he must have felt both guilt and panic about his lack of progress on *Answered Prayers.* In the last few years he seemed intent on fooling not only me and other close friends about his work on it, but even the public at large; at least twice he announced to interviewers that he had just completed the

---

Blood corrected by the author; a few pictures; many newspaper clippings; notebooks containing interviews of the characters in *In Cold Blood;* copies or galleys of other magazines *(Esquire, Redbook, Mademoiselle, McCall's)* in which his articles or stories had appeared; half a dozen letters—and a few pages of early notes about *Answered Prayers.* In 1985 all of this was donated to the New York Public Library by the Capote estate, and today it can be seen by scholars in the Rare Books and Manuscripts Division at the Central Research Library at 42nd Street.

book, had handed it in to Random House and that it would be published within six months. Thereafter our publicity department and I would be inundated with a flurry of calls, to which we could only reply that we hadn't seen the manuscript. Clearly Truman must have been desperate.

The last factor in the erosion of our relationship was Truman's mounting dependence on alcohol and drugs from 1977 on. I now realize that I was not as sympathetic about his plight as I should have been; instead I focused on the waste of talent, on his self-deceptions, on his endless ramblings, on the unintelligible 1:00 A.M. phone calls—and above all on the loss of my delightful, witty and mischievous companion of those first sixteen years whom I selfishly mourned more than I did his increasing pain.

There are three theories about the missing chapters of *Answered Prayers*. The first has it that the manuscript was completed and is either stashed in a safe-deposit box somewhere, was seized by an ex-lover for malice or for profit, or even—the latest rumor—that Truman kept it in a locker in the Los Angeles Greyhound Bus Depot. But with every passing day these scenarios seem less plausible.

The second theory is that after the publication of "Kate McCloud" in 1976 Truman never wrote another line of the book, perhaps partly because he was devastated by the public—and private—reaction to those chapters, perhaps partly because he came to realize that it would never achieve those Proustian standards he had set for himself. This theory is compelling for at least one reason: Jack Dunphy, Truman's closest friend and companion for over thirty years, believes it. Still, Truman rarely discussed his work with Jack, and in the last years they were apart more often than they were together.

A third theory, to which I hesitantly subscribe, is that Truman did indeed write at least some of the above-mentioned chapters (probably "A Severe Insult to the Brain" and "Father Flanagan's All-Night Nigger-Queen Kosher Café"), but at some point in the early 1980's deliberately destroyed them. In favor of this theory, at least four friends of Truman claim to have read (or had had read aloud to them by the author) one or two chapters besides the three that appear here. Certainly he convinced me that more of the manuscript existed; over and over again at lunch during the last six years of his life, when he was often almost incoherent because of drugs or alcohol or both, he discussed the four missing titled chapters with me in great detail, even to the point of quoting lines of dialogue which were always identical even when he recited them months or even years apart. The pattern was always the same: when I asked to see the chapter in question he would promise to send it around the next day. At the end of that day I would call and Truman would say he was having it retyped and would send it over on Monday; on the Monday afternoon his phone would not answer and he would disappear for a week or more.

I subscribe to this third theory not so much out of a reluctance to admit my gullibility, but because Truman was so convincing in his description of those chapters. Of course it is possible that those lines existed only in his head, but it is hard to believe that at some point he did not put them down on paper. He had great pride in his work, but also an unusual objectivity about it, and my suspicion is that at some point he destroyed every vestige of whatever chapters he'd written other than the three in this volume.

There is only one person who knows the truth, and he is dead. God bless him.

JOSEPH M. FOX

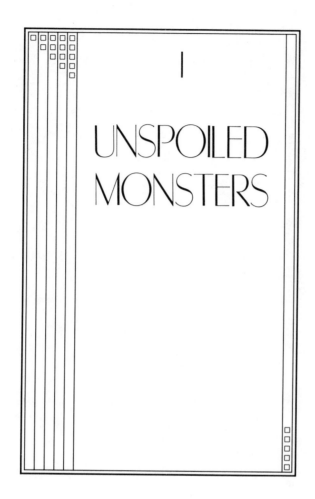

I

UNSPOILED
MONSTERS

*S*omewhere in this world there exists an exceptional philosopher named Florie Rotondo.

The other day I came across one of her ruminations printed in a magazine devoted to the writings of schoolchildren. It said: *If I could do anything, I would go to the middle of our planet, Earth, and seek uranium, rubies, and gold. I'd look for Unspoiled Monsters. Then I'd move to the country. Florie Rotondo, age eight.*

Florie, honey, I know just what you mean—even if you don't: how could you, age eight?

Because I have *been* to the middle of our planet; at any rate, have suffered the tribulations such a journey might inflict. I have searched for uranium, rubies, gold, and, en route, have observed others in these pursuits. And listen, Florie—I have met Unspoiled Monsters! Spoiled ones, too. But the *un*spoiled variety is the rara avis: white truffles compared to black; bitter wild asparagus as

3

opposed to garden-grown. The one thing I haven't done is move to the country.

As a matter of fact, I am writing this on Y.M.C.A. stationery in a Manhattan Y.M.C.A., where I have been existing the last month in a viewless second-floor cell. I'd prefer the sixth floor— so if I decided to climb out the window, it would make a vital difference. Perhaps I'll change rooms. Ascend. Probably not. I'm a coward. But not cowardly enough to take the plunge.

My name is P. B. Jones, and I'm of two minds—whether to tell you something about myself right now, or wait and weave the information into the text of the tale. I could just as well tell you nothing, or very little, for I consider myself a reporter in this matter, not a participant, at least not an important one. But maybe it's easier to start with me.

As I say, I'm called P. B. Jones; I am either thirty-five or thirty-six: the reason for the uncertainty is that no one knows when I was born or who my parents were. All we know is that I was a baby abandoned in the balcony of a St. Louis vaudeville theater. This happened 20 January 1936. Catholic nuns raised me in an austere red-stone orphanage that dominated an embankment overlooking the Mississippi River.

I was a favorite of the nuns, for I was a bright kid and a beauty; they never realized how conniving I was, duplicitous, or how much I despised their drabness, their aroma: incense and dishwater, candles and creosote, white sweat. One of the sisters, Sister Martha, I rather liked, she taught English and was so convinced

4

I had a gift for writing that I became convinced of it myself. All the same, when I left the orphanage, ran away, I didn't leave her a note or ever communicate with her again: a typical sample of my numbed, opportunistic nature.

Hitchhiking, and with no particular destination in mind, I was picked up by a man driving a white Cadillac convertible. A burly guy with a broken nose and a flushed, freckled Irish complexion. Nobody you'd take for a queer. But he was. He asked where I was headed, and I just shrugged; he wanted to know how old I was —I said eighteen, though really I was three years younger. He grinned and said: "Well, I wouldn't want to corrupt the morals of a minor."

As if I *had* any morals.

Then he said, solemnly: "You're a good-looking kid." True: on the short side, five seven (eventually five eight), but sturdy and well-proportioned, with curly brown-blond hair, green-flecked brown eyes, and a face dramatically angular; to examine myself in a mirror was always a reassuring experience. So when Ned took his dive, he thought he was grabbing cherry. Ho ho! Starting at an early age, seven or eight or thereabouts, I'd run the gamut with many an older boy and several priests and also a handsome Negro gardener. In fact, I was a kind of Hershey Bar whore— there wasn't much I wouldn't do for a nickel's worth of chocolate.

Though I lived with him for several months, I can't remember Ned's last name. Ames? He was chief masseur at a big Miami Beach hotel—one of those ice-cream-color Hebrew hangouts with a French name. Ned taught me the trade, and after I left him I earned my living as a masseur at a succession of Miami Beach hotels. Also, I had a number of private clients, men and women I massaged and trained in figure and facial exercises—although facial exercises are a lot of crap; the only effective one is cocksucking. No joke, there's nothing like it for firming the jawline.

With my assistance, Agnes Beerbaum improved her facial contours admirably. Mrs. Beerbaum was the widow of a Detroit dentist who had retired to Fort Lauderdale, where he promptly experienced a fatal coronary. She was not rich, but she had money —along with an ailing back. It was to alleviate these spinal spasms that I first entered her life, and remained in it long enough to accumulate, through gifts above my usual fee, over ten thousand dollars.

Now *that's* when I should have moved to the country.

But I bought a ticket on a Greyhound bus that carried me to New York. I had one suitcase, and it contained very little—only underwear, shirts, a bathroom kit, and numerous notebooks in which I had scribbled poems and a few short stories. I was eighteen, it was October, and I've always remembered the October glitter of Manhattan as my bus approached across the stinking New Jersey marshes. As Thomas Wolfe, a once-admired and now-forgotten idol, might have written: Oh, what promise those windows held!—cold and fiery in the rippling shine of a tumbling autumn sun.

Since then, I've fallen in love with many cities, but only an

6

orgasm lasting an hour could surpass the bliss of my first year in New York. Unfortunately, I decided to marry.

Perhaps what I wanted in the way of a wife was the city itself, my happiness there, my sense of inevitable fame, fortune. Alas, what I married was a girl. This bloodless, fishbelly-pale amazon with roped yellow hair and egglike lilac eyes. She was a fellow student at Columbia University, where I had enrolled in a creative-writing class taught by Martha Foley, one of the founder/editors of the old magazine *Story*. What I liked about Hulga (yes, I know Flannery O'Connor named one of her heroines Hulga, but I'm not swiping; it's simply coincidence) was that she never wearied of listening to me read my work aloud. Mostly, the content of my stories was the opposite of my character—that is, they were tender and *triste;* but Hulga thought they were beautiful, and her great lilac eyes always gratifyingly brimmed and trickled at the end of a reading.

Soon after we were married, I discovered there was a fine reason why her eyes had such a marvelous moronic serenity. She was a moron. Or damn near. Certainly she wasn't playing with a full deck. Good old humorless hulking Hulga, yet so dainty and mincingly clean—housewifey. She hadn't a clue how I really felt about her, not until Christmas, when her parents came to visit us: a pair of Swedish brutes from Minnesota, a mammoth twosome twice the size of their daughter. We were living in a one-and-a-half-room apartment near Morningside Heights. Hulga had bought a sort of Rockefeller Center-type tree: it spread floor to ceiling and wall to wall—the damn thing was sucking the oxygen out of the air. And the fuss she made over it, the fortune she spent on this Woolworth's shit! I happen to hate Christmas because, if you'll pardon the tearjerker note, it always amounted to the year's most depressing episode in my Missouri orphanage. So on Christmas Eve, minutes before Hulga's parents were supposed to arrive for the Yuletide hoedown, I abruptly lost control: took the tree apart and piece by piece fed it out the window in a blaze of blown fuses and smashing bulbs—Hulga the whole while hollering like a half-slaughtered hog. (Attention, students of literature! Alliteration—have you noticed?—is my least vice.) Told her what I thought of her, too—and for once those eyes lost their idiot purity.

Presently, Mama and Papa appeared, the Minnesota giants: sounds like a homicidal hockey team, which is how they reacted. Hulga's folks simply slammed me back and forth between them —and before I conked out, they had cracked five ribs, splintered a shinbone, and blackened both eyes. Then, apparently, the giants packed up their kid and headed home. I've never heard a word from Hulga, not in all the years that have gone by; but, so far as I know, we are still legally attached.

Are you familiar with the term "killer fruit"? It's a certain kind of queer who has Freon refrigerating his bloodstream. Diaghilev, for example. J. Edgar Hoover. Hadrian. Not to compare him with those pedestal personages, but the fellow I'm thinking of is Turner Boatwright—Boaty, as his courtiers called him.

Mr. Boatwright was the fiction editor of a women's fashion magazine that published "quality" writers. He came to my attention, or rather I came to his, when one day he spoke to our writing class. I was sitting in the front row, and I could tell, by the way his chilly crotch-watching eyes kept gravitating toward me, what was spinning around in his pretty curly-grey head. Okay, but I decided he wasn't going to get any bargain. After class, the students gathered around to meet him. Not me; I left without waiting to be introduced. A month passed, during which I polished the two stories of mine I considered best: "Suntan," which was about beachboy whores in Miami Beach, and "Massage," which concerned the humiliations of a dentist's widow grovelingly in love with a teen-age masseur.

Manuscripts in hand, I went to call on Mr. Boatwright—without an appointment; I simply went to the offices of the magazine and asked the receptionist to tell Mr. Boatwright that one of Miss Foley's students was there to see him. I was certain he would know which one. But when I was eventually escorted into his office, he pretended not to remember me. I wasn't fooled.

The office was not unbusinesslike; it seemed a Victorian parlor. Mr. Boatwright was seated in a cane rocking chair beside a table draped with fringed shawls that served as a desk; another rocker was placed on the opposite side of the table. The editor, with a sleepy gesture meant to disguise cobra alertness, motioned me toward it (his own chair, as I later discovered, contained a little pillow with an embroidered inscription: MOTHER). Although it was a sizzling spring day, the window curtains, heavy velvet and of a hue I believe is called puce, were drawn; the only light came from a pair of student lamps, one with dark red shades, the other with green. An interesting place, Mr. Boatwright's lair; clearly the management gave him great leeway.

"Well, Mr. Jones?"

I explained my errand, said I had been impressed by his lecture at Columbia, by the sincerity of his desire to assist young authors, and announced that I had brought two short stories that I wished to submit for his consideration.

He said, his voice scary with cute sarcasm: "And why did you choose to submit them in person? The customary method is by mail."

I smiled, and my smile is an ingratiating proposition; indeed, it is usually construed as one. "I was afraid you would never read them. An unknown writer without an agent? I shouldn't think too many such stories ever reach you."

"They do if they have merit. My assistant, Miss Shaw, is an exceedingly able and perceptive reader. How old are you?"

"I'll be twenty in August."

"And you think you're a genius?"

"I don't know." Which was untrue; I was certain I was. "That's why I'm here. I'd like your opinion."

"I'll say this: you're ambitious. Or is it just plain push? What are you, a yid?"

My reply was no particular credit to me; though I am relatively without self-pity (well, I wonder), I've never been above exploiting my background to achieve sympathetic advantage. "Possibly. I was raised in an orphanage. I never knew my parents."

Nevertheless, the gentleman had knee-punched me with aching accuracy. He had my number; I was no longer so sure I had his. At the time I was immune to the mechanical vices—seldom smoked, never drank. But now, without permission, I selected a cigarette from a nearby tortoise-shell box; as I lighted it, all the matches in the matchbook exploded. A tiny bonfire erupted in my hand. I jumped up, wringing my hand and whimpering.

My host merely and coolly pointed at the fallen, still-flaming matches. He said: "Careful. Stamp that out. You'll damage the carpet." Then: "Come here. Give me your hand."

His lips parted. Slowly his mouth absorbed my index finger, the one most scorched. He plunged the finger into the depths of his mouth, almost withdrew, plunged again—like a huntsman drawing dangerous liquid from a snakebite. Stopping, he asked: "There. Is that better?"

The seesaw had upended; a transference of power had occurred, or so I was foolish enough to believe.

"Much; thank you."

"Very well," he said, rising to bolt the office door. "Now we shall continue the treatment."

No, it wasn't as easy as that. Boaty was a hard fellow; if necessary, he would have paid for his pleasures, but he never would have published one of my stories. Of the original two I gave him, he said: "They're not good. Ordinarily, I'd never encourage anyone with a talent as limited as yours. That is the cruelest thing anyone can do—to encourage someone to believe he has gifts he actually doesn't possess. However, you do have a certain word sense. Feeling for characterization. Perhaps something can be made of it. If you're willing to risk it, take the chance of ruining your life, I'll help you. But I don't recommend it."

I wish I had listened to him. I wish that then and there I had moved to the country. But it was too late, for I had already started my journey to the Earth's interior.

Am running out of paper. I think I'll take a shower. And afterward I may move to the sixth floor.

I have moved to the sixth floor.

However, my window is flat against the next-door building; even if I did step over the sill, I'd only bump my head. We're having a September heat wave, and my room is so small, so hot, that I have to leave my door open day and night, which is unfortunate because, as in most Young Men's Christian Associations, the corridors murmur with the slippered footfalls of libidinous Christians; if you leave your door open, it's frequently understood as an invitation. Not from me, no sir.

The other day, when I started this account, I had no notion whether or not I'd continue it. However, I've just come from a drugstore, where I purchased a box of Blackwing pencils, a pencil sharpener, and a half-dozen thick copybooks. Anyway, I've nothing better to do. Except look for a job. Only, I don't know what kind of work to look for—unless I went back to massage. I'm not fit for much anymore. And, to be honest, I keep thinking that maybe, if I change most of the names, I could publish this as a novel. Hell, I've nothing to lose; of course, a couple of people might try to kill me, but I'd consider that a favor.

After I'd submitted more than twenty stories, Boaty did buy one. He edited it to the bone and half rewrote it himself, but at least I was in print. "Many Thoughts of Morton," by P. B. Jones. It was about a nun in love with a Negro gardener named Morton (the same gardener who had been in love with me). It attracted attention, and was reprinted in that year's *Best American Short Stories;* more importantly, it was noticed by a distinguished friend of Boaty's, Miss Alice Lee Langman.

Boaty owned a roomy old brownstone town house; it was far east in the upper Eighties. The interior was an exaggerated replica of his office, a crimson Victorian horsehair mélange: beaded curtains and stuffed owls frowning under glass bells. This brand of camp, now *démodé,* was amusingly uncommon in those days, and Boaty's parlor was one of Manhattan's most populated social centers.

I met Jean Cocteau there—a walking laser light with a sprig of *muguet* in his buttonhole; he asked if I was tattooed, and when I said no, his overly intelligent eyes glazed and glided elsewhere.

Both Dietrich and Garbo occasionally came to Boaty's, the latter always escorted by Cecil Beaton, whom I'd met when he photographed me for Boaty's magazine (an overheard exchange between these two: Beaton, "The most distressing fact of growing older is that I find my private parts are shrinking." Garbo, after a mournful pause, "Ah, if only I could say the same").

In truth, one encountered an exceptional share of the celebrated at Boaty's, performers as various as Martha Graham and Gypsy Rose Lee, sequined sorts interspersed with an array of painters (Tchelitchew, Cadmus, Rivers, Warhol, Rauschenberg), composers (Bernstein, Copland, Britten, Barber, Blitzstein, Diamond, Menotti) and, most plentifully, writers (Auden, Isherwood, Wescott, Mailer, Williams, Styron, Porter, and, on several occasions, when he was in New York, the Lolita-minded Faulkner, usually grave and courtly under the double weight of uncertain gentility and a Jack Daniel's hangover). Also, Alice Lee Langman, whom Boaty considered America's first lady of letters.

To all these people, the living among them, I must by now be the merest memory. If that. Of course, Boaty would have remembered me, though not with pleasure (I can well imagine what he might say: "P. B. Jones? That tramp. No doubt he's peddling his ass to elderly Arab buggers in the souks of Marrakech"); but Boaty is gone, beaten to death in his mahogany house by a heroincrazed Puerto Rican hustler who left him with both eyeballs unhinged and dangling down his cheeks.

And Alice Lee Langman died last year.

The New York Times printed her obituary on the front page, accompanied by the famous photograph of her made by Arnold Genthe in Berlin in 1927. Creative females are not often presentable. Look at Mary McCarthy!—so frequently advertised as a Great Beauty. Alice Lee Langman, however, was a swan among the swans of our century: a peer of Cléo de Mérode, the Marquesa de Casa Maury, Garbo, Barbara Cushing Paley, the three Wyndham sisters, Diana Dudd Cooper, Lena Horne, Richard Finnochio (the transvestite who calls himself Harlow), Gloria Guinness, Maya Plisetskaya, Marilyn Monroe, and lastly, the incomparable Kate McCloud. There have been several intellectual lesbians of physical distinction: Colette, Gertrude Stein, Willa Cather, Ivy Compton-Burnett, Carson McCullers, Jane Bowles; and, in altogether another category, simple endearing prettiness, both Eleanor Clark and Katherine Anne Porter deserve their reputations.

But Alice Lee Langman was a perfected presence, an enameled lady marked with the androgynous quality, that sexually ambivalent aura that seems a common denominator among certain persons whose allure crosses all frontiers—a mystique not confined to women, for Nureyev has it, Nehru had it, so did the youthful Marlon Brando and Elvis Presley, so did Montgomery Clift and James Dean.

When I met Miss Langman, and I never called her anything else, she was far into her late fifties, yet she looked eerily unaltered from her long-ago Genthe portrait. The author of *Wild Asparagus* and *Five Black Guitars* had eyes the color of Anatolian waters, and her hair, a sleek silvery blue, was brushed straight back, fitting her erect head like an airy cap. Her nose was reminiscent of Pavlova's: prominent, slightly irregular. She was pale, with a healthy pallor, an apple-whiteness, and when she spoke she was difficult to understand, for her voice, unlike most women of Dixie origin, was neither high nor rapid (only Southern men *drawl*), but was muted, as cello-contralto as a mourning dove's.

She said, that first night at Boaty's: "Would you see me home? I hear thunder, and I'm afraid of it."

She was not afraid of thunder, nor of anything else—except unreturned love and commercial success. Miss Langman's exquisite renown, while justified, was founded on one novel and three short-story collections, none of them much bought or read outside academia and the pastures of the cognoscenti. Like the value of diamonds, her prestige depended upon a controlled and limited output; and, in those terms, she was a royal success, the queen of the writer-in-residence swindle, the prizes racket, the high-honorarium con, the grants-in-aid-to-struggling-artists shit. Everybody, the Ford Foundation, the Guggenheim Foundation, the National Institute of Arts and Letters, the National Council on the Arts, the Library of Congress, et al., was hell-bound to gorge her with tax-free greenery, and Miss Langman, like those circus midgets who lose their living if they grow an inch or two, was ever aware her prestige would collapse if the ordinary public began to read and reward her. Meanwhile, she was raking in the charity chips like a croupier—enough to afford an apartment on Park Avenue, small but stylish.

Having followed a sedate Tennessee childhood—suitable to the daughter of a Methodist minister, which she was—with a kickup that included bohemian duty in Berlin and Shanghai as well as in Paris and Havana, and having had four husbands, one of them a twenty-year-old surfboarding beauty she had met while lecturing at Berkeley, Miss Langman had now relapsed, at least in material matters, into the ancestral values she may have misplaced but never lost.

Retrospectively, with knowledge since acquired, I can appreciate the distinction of Miss Langman's apartment. At the time I thought it cold and underdone. The "soft" furniture was covered in a crisp linen as white as the pictureless walls; the floors were highly polished and uncarpeted. Only white jardinieres massed with fresh green leaves interrupted the snowiness of the interior; those, and several signed pieces, among them an opulently severe partner's desk and a fine set of rosewood book cabinets. "I would prefer," Miss Langman told me, "to own two really good forks rather than a dozen that are merely good. That's why these rooms are so little furnished. I can live only with the best, but I can't finance enough of it to live with. Anyway, clutter is alien to my nature. Give me an empty beach on a winter's day when the water is very still. I'd go mad in a house like Boaty's."

Miss Langman was often, in interviews, described as a witty conversationalist; how can a woman be witty when she hasn't a sense of humor?—and she had none, which was her central flaw as a person and as an artist. But she was indeed a talker: a relentless bedroom back-seat driver: "No, Billy. Leave your shirt on and don't take off your socks the first man I ever saw he was in just his shirt and socks. Mr. Billy Langman. The Reverend Billy. And there's something about it a man with his socks on and his billy up and ready here Billy take this pillow and put it under my that's it that's right that's good ah Billy that's *good* good as Natasha I had a thing once with a Russian Dyke Natasha worked at the Russian Embassy in Warsaw and she was always hungry she liked to hide a cherry down there and eat ah Billy I can't I *can't* take that without withoutso slide up honey and suck my that's it that's it let me hold your billy but Billy why aren't you more! well! more!"

Why? Because I am one of those persons who, when sexually immersed, require serious silence, the hush of impeccable concentration. Perhaps it is due to my pubescent training as a Hershey Bar whore, and because I have consistently willed myself to accommodate unscintillating partners—whatever the reason, for me to reach an edge and fall over, all the mechanics must be assisted by the deepest fantasizing, an intoxicating mental cinema that does not welcome lovemaking chatter.

The truth is, I am rarely with the person I am with, so to say; and I'm sure that many of us, even most of us, share this condition of dependence upon an inner scenery, imagined and remembered erotic fragments, shadows irrelevant to the body above or beneath us—those images our minds accept inside sexual seizure but exclude once the beast has been routed, for, regardless of how tolerant we are, these cameos are intolerable to the meanspirited watchmen within us. "That's better better and better Billy let me have billy now that's uh uh uh it that's *it* only slower slower and slower now hard hard hit it hard ay ay *los cojones* let me hear them ring now slower slower dradraaaaagdrag it out now hit hard hard ay ay daddy Jesus have mercy Jesus Jesus goddamdaddyamighty come with me Billy come! come!" How can I, when the lady won't let me concentrate on areas more provocative than her roaring roiling undisciplined persona? "Let's hear it, let's hear them ring": thus the grande mademoiselle of the cultural press as she bucked her way through a sixty-second sequence of multiple triumphs. Off I went to the bathroom, stretched out in the cold dry bathtub and, thinking the thoughts necessary to me (just as Miss Langman, in the private quietude beneath her public turbulence, had been absorbed in hers: recalling . . . a girlhood? overly effective glimpses of the Reverend Billy? naked except for his shirt and socks? or a honeyed womanly tongue lollipopping away some wintry afternoon? or a pasta-bellied whale-whanged wop picked up in Palermo and hog-fucked a hot Sicilian infinity ago?), masturbated.

I have a friend, who isn't queer but dislikes women, and he has said: "The only women I've got any use for are Mrs. Fist and her five daughters." There is much to be said for Mrs. Fist—she is hygienic, never makes scenes, costs nothing, is utterly loyal and always at hand when needed.

"Thank you," Miss Langman said when I returned. "Amazing, someone your age to know all that. To have such confidence. I had thought I was accepting a pupil, but it would seem he has nothing to learn."

The last sentence is stylistically characteristic—direct, felt, yet a bit *enunciated,* literary. Nevertheless, I could more than see how valuable and flattering it was for an ambitious young writer to be the protégé of Alice Lee Langman, and so presently I went to live in the Park Avenue apartment. Boaty, upon hearing of it, and because he didn't dare oppose Miss Langman but all the same wanted to bitch it up, telephoned her and said: "Alice, I'm only saying this because you met the creature in my house. I feel responsible. Watch out! He'll go with anything—mules, men, dogs, fire hydrants. Just yesterday I had a furious letter from Jean [Cocteau]. From Paris. He spent a night with our amigo in the Plaza Hotel. And now he has the clap to prove it! God knows what the creature's crawling with. Best see your doctor. And one thing more: the boy's a thief. He's stolen over five hundred dollars forging checks in my name. I could have him jailed tomorrow." Some of this might have been true, though none of it was; but see what I mean by a killer fruit?

Not that it mattered; it wouldn't have fazed Miss Langman if Boaty could have proved I was a swindler who had swindled a hunchbacked pair of Soviet Siamese twins out of their last ruble. She was in love with me, she said so, and I believed her; one night, when her voice waved and dipped from too much red and yellow wine, she asked—oh in such a whimper-simper stupid-touching way you wanted to knock out her teeth but maybe kiss her, too —whether I loved her; as I'm naught if not a liar, I told her sure. Happily, I've suffered the full horrors of love only once—you will hear about it when the time comes; that's a promise. However, to revert to the Langman tragedy. Is it—I'm not certain—possible to love someone if your first interest is the use you can make of him? Doesn't the gainful motive, and the guilt accruing to it, halt the progression of other emotions? It can be argued that even the most decently coupled people were initially magnetized by the mutual-exploitation principle—sex, shelter, appeased ego; but still that is trivial, human: the difference between that and truly *using* another person is the difference between edible mushrooms and the kind that kill: Unspoiled Monsters.

What I wanted from Miss Langman was: her agent, her publisher, her name attached to a Holy Roller critique of my work in one of those moldy but academically influential quarterlies. These objectives were, in time, achieved and dazzlingly added to. As a result of her prestigious interventions, P. B. Jones was soon the recipient of a Guggenheim Fellowship ($3,000), a grant from the National Institute of Arts and Letters ($1,000), and a publisher's advance against a book of short stories ($2,000). Moreover, Miss Langman prepared these stories, nine of them, groomed them to a champion-show finish, then reviewed them, *Answered Prayers and Other Stories*, once in *Partisan Review* and again in *The New York Times Book Review*. The title was her decision;

though there was no story called "Answered Prayers," she said: "It's very fitting. St. Teresa of Avila commented, 'More tears are shed over answered prayers than unanswered ones.' Perhaps that isn't the precise quotation, but we can look it up. The point is, the theme moving through your work, as nearly as I can locate it, is of people achieving a desperate aim only to have it rebound upon them—accentuating, and accelerating, their desperation."

Prophetically, *Answered Prayers* answered none of mine. By the time the book appeared, many key figures in the literary apparatus considered that Miss Langman had oversponsored her Baby Gigolo (Boaty's description; he also told everyone: "Poor Alice. It's *Chéri* and *La Fin de Chéri* rolled into one!"), even felt she had displayed a lack of integrity appalling in so scrupulous an artist.

I can't claim my stories were one with those of Turgenev and Flaubert, but certainly they were honorable enough not to be entirely ignored. No one attacked them; it would have been better if someone had, less painful than this grey rejecting void that numbed and nauseated and started one thirsting for martinis before noon. Miss Langman was as anguished as I—sharing my disappointment, so she said, but secretly it was because she suspected the sweet waters of her own crystalline reputation had been seweraged.

I can't forget her sitting there in her perfect-taste parlor, with gin and tears reddening her beautiful eyes, nodding, nodding, nodding, absorbing every word of my mean gin-inspired assaults, the blame I heaped on her for the book's debacle, my defeat, my cold hell; nodding, nodding, biting her lips, suppressing any hint of retaliation, accepting it because she was as strong in the sureness of her gifts as I was feeble and paranoid in the uncertainty of mine, and because she knew one swift true sentence from her would be lethal—and because she was afraid if I left, it would indeed be the last of *any chéri.*

Old Texas saying: Women are like rattlesnakes—the last thing that dies is their tail.

Some women, all their lives, will put up with anything for a fuck; and Miss Langman, so I'm told, was an enthusiast until a stroke killed her. However, as Kate McCloud has said: "A really good lay is worth a trip around the world—in more ways than one." And Kate McCloud, as we all know, has earned an opinion: Christ, if Kate had as many pricks sticking out of her as she's had stuck in her, she'd look like a porcupine.

But Miss Langman, R.I.P., had completed her segment in The Story of P. B. Jones—A Paranoid Release in Association with Priapus Productions; for P. B. had already encountered the future. His name was Denham Fouts—Denny, as his friends called him, among them Christopher Isherwood and Gore Vidal, both of whom, after his death, impaled him as a principal character in works of their own, Vidal in his story "Pages from an Abandoned Journal" and Isherwood in a novel, *Down There on a Visit.*

Denny, long before he surfaced in my cove, was a legend well-known to me, a myth entitled: Best-Kept Boy in the World.

When Denny was sixteen, he was living in a Florida crossroads cracker town and working in a bakery owned by his father. Rescue—some might say ruin—arrived one morning in the fattish form of a millionaire driving a brand-new built-to-order 1936 Duesenberg convertible. The fellow was a cosmetics tycoon whose fortune largely depended upon a celebrated suntan lotion; he had been married twice, but his preference was Ganymedes between the ages of fourteen and seventeen. When he saw Denny, it must have been as though a collector of antique porcelain had strayed into a junkshop and discovered a Meissen "white swan" service: the shock! the greedy chill! He bought doughnuts, invited Denny for a spin in the Duesenberg, even offered him command of the wheel; and that night, without having returned home for even a change of underwear, Denny was a hundred miles away in Miami. A month later his grieving parents, who had despaired after sending searching parties through the local swamps, received a letter postmarked Paris, France. The letter became the first entry in a many-volumed scrapbook: *The Universal Travels of Our Son Denham Fouts.*

Paris, Tunis, Berlin, Capri, St. Moritz, Budapest, Belgrade, Cap Ferrat, Biarritz, Venice, Athens, Istanbul, Moscow, Morocco, Estoril, London, Bombay, Calcutta, London, London, Paris, Paris, Paris—and his original proprietor had been left far behind, oh, away back yonder in Capri, honey; for it was in Capri that Denny caught the eye of and absconded with a seventy-year-old great-grandfather, who was also a director of Dutch Petroleum. This gentleman lost Denny to royalty—Prince Paul, later King Paul, of Greece. The prince was much nearer Denny's age, and the affection between them was fairly balanced, so much so that once they visited a tattooist in Vienna and had themselves identically marked—a small blue insignia above the heart, though I can't remember what it was or what it signified.

Nor can I recall how the affair ended, other than that The End was a quarrel caused by Denny's sniffing cocaine in the bar of the Hotel Beau Rivage in Lausanne. But by now Denny, like Porfiro Rubirosa, another word-of-mouth myth on the Continental circuit, had generated the successful adventurer's *sine qua non:* mystery and a popular desire to examine the source of it. For example, both Doris Duke and Barbara Hutton had, in effect, paid a million dollars to find out if other ladies were lying when they praised that kinky-haired piece of trade His Excellency the Dominican Ambassador Porfirio Rubirosa, groaning over the fat effectiveness of that quadroon cock, a purported eleven-inch café-au-lai sinker thick as a man's wrist (according to spinners who had spun them both, the ambassador's only peer in the pecker parade was the Shah of Iran). As for the good late Prince Aly Khan—who was a straight dealer and a fine friend to Kate McCloud—as for Aly, the only thing that Feydeau-farce brigade shuffling through his bed sheets really wanted to know was: is it true this stud can go an hour a time five times a day and never come? I'm assuming you know the answer; but if you don't, it's yes—an Oriental trick, virtually a conjurer's stunt, called *karezza,* and the dominant ingredient is not spermatic stamina but imagistic control: one sucks and fucks while firmly picturing a plain brown box or a trotting dog. Of course, one ought also to be always stuffed with oysters and caviar and have no occupation that would interfere with eating and snoring and concentrating on plain brown boxes.

Women experimented with Denny: the Honorable Daisy Fellowes, the American Singer Sewing Machine heiress, lugged him around the Aegean aboard her crisp little yacht, the *Sister Anne;* but the principal contributors to Denny's Geneva bank account continued to be the richest of the double-gaited big daddies—a Chilean among *le tout Paris,* Arturo Lopez-Willshaw, our planet's chief supplier of guano, fossilized bird shit, and the Marquis de Cuevas, road-company Diaghilev. But in 1938, on a visit to London, Denny found his final and permanent patron: Peter Watson, heir of an oleomargarine tycoon, was not just another rich queen, but—in a stooped, intellectual, bitter-lipped style—one of the most personable men in England. It was his money that started and supported Cyril Connolly's magazine *Horizon.* Watson's circle was dismayed when their rather severe friend, who had usually shown a conventional regard for simple sailor boys, became infatuated with the notorious Denny Fouts, an "exhibitionistic playboy," a drug addict, an American who talked as though his mouth were busy with a pound of Alabama corn mush.

But one had to have experienced Denny's stranglehold, a pressure that brought the victim teasingly close to an ultimate slumber, to appreciate its allure. Denny was suited to only one role,

The Beloved, for that was all he had ever been. So, except for his sporadic barterings with maritime trade, had this Watson been The Beloved, a besieged fellow whose conduct toward his admirers contained touches beyond De Sade (once Watson deliberately set forth on a sea voyage halfway round the world with an aristocratic, love-besotted young man whom he punished by never permitting a kiss or caress, though night after night they slept in the same narrow bed—that is, Mr. Watson slept while his perfectly decent but disintegrating friend twitched with insomnia and an aching scrotum).

Of course, as is true of most men sadistically streaked, Watson had paralleling masochistic impulses; but it took Denny, with his *púttána*'s instinct for an ashamed client's unspoken needs, to divine this and act accordingly. Once the tables are turned, only a humiliator can appreciate humiliation's sweeter edges: Watson was in love with Denny's cruelty, for Watson was an artist recognizing the work of a superior artist, labors that left the quinine-elegant Mr. W. stretched in stark-awake comas of jealousy and delicious despair. The Beloved even used his drug addiction to sado-romantic advantage, for Watson, while forced to supply the money that supported a habit he deplored, was convinced that only his love and attention could rescue The Beloved from a heroin grave. When The Beloved truly desired a turn of the screw, he had merely to turn to his medicine chest.

Apparently it was concern for Denny's welfare that led Watson to insist, in 1940, at the start of the German bombing, that Denny

leave London and return to the United States—a journey Denny
made chaperoned by Cyril Connolly's American wife, Jean. The
latter couple never met again—Jean Connolly, a bountiful,
biological sort, passed out and on in the aftermath of a rollick-
ing soldier-sailor-marine-marijuana-saturated Denny-Jean cross-
country high-jinks hegira.

Denny spent the war years in California, several of them as a
prisoner in a camp for conscientious objectors; but it was early on
in the California days that he met Christopher Isherwood, who
was working in Hollywood as a film scenarist. Here, quoting
from the previously mentioned Isherwood novel, which I looked
up at the public library this morning, is how he describes Denny
(or Paul, as he calls him): "When I first set eyes on Paul, as he
entered the restaurant, I remember I noticed his strangely erect
walk; he seemed almost paralytic with tension. He was always
slim, but then he looked boyishly skinny, and he was dressed like
a boy in his teens, with an exaggerated air of innocence which he
seemed to be daring us to challenge. His drab black suit, narrow-
chested and without shoulder padding, clean white shirt and plain
black tie, made him look as if he had just arrived in town from
a strictly religious boarding school. His dressing so young didn't
strike me as ridiculous, because it went with his appearance. Yet,
since I knew he was in his late twenties, this youthfulness itself
had a slightly sinister effect, like something uncannily preserved."

Seven years later, when I arrived to live at 33 rue du Bac, the
address of a Left Bank apartment Peter Watson owned in Paris,

the Denham Fouts I encountered there, though paler than his favorite ivory opium pipe, was not much changed from Herr Issyvoo's California friend: he still looked vulnerably young, as though youth were a chemical solution in which Fouts was permanently incarcerated.

How was it, though, that P. B. Jones found himself in Paris, a guest in the high-ceilinged dusk of those shuttered, meandering rooms?

One moment, please: I'm going downstairs to the showers. For the seventh day, Manhattan's heat has hit ninety or higher.

Some of our establishment's Christian satyrs shower so frequently and loiter so long they look like water-logged Kewpie dolls; but they are young and, by and large, well formed. However, the most obsessed of these hygienic sex fiends, and a relentless shuffle-shuffle hunter-haunter of the dormitory corridors as well, is an old guy nicknamed Gums. He limps, he's blind in his left eye, a runny sore persists at the corner of his mouth, pockmarks pit his skin like some diabolic, pestilential tattoo. Just now he brushed his hand against my thigh, and I pretended not to notice; yet the touch created an irritating sensation, as though his fingers were splints of burning nettle.

Answered Prayers had been out several months when I received from Paris a terse note: "Dear Mr. Jones, Your stories are brilliant. So is Cecil Beaton's portrait. Please join me here as my guest.

Enclosed is a first-class passage aboard the Queen Elizabeth, sailing New York-LeHavre April 24. If you require a reference, ask Beaton: he is an old acquaintance. Sincerely, Denham Fouts."

As I've said, I'd heard a lot about Mr. Fouts—enough to know it was not my literary style that had stimulated his daring missive but the photograph of me Beaton had taken for Boaty's magazine and which I had used on the jacket of my book. Later, when I knew Denny, I understood what it was in that face that had so traumatized him he was ready to chance his invitation and underwrite it with a gift he could not afford—*could* not because he'd been deserted by a fed-to-the-teeth Peter Watson, was living in Watson's Paris apartment on a day-to-day squatter's-rights basis, and existing on scattered handouts from loyal friends and old, semi-blackmailed suitors. The photograph conveyed a notion of me altogether incorrect—a crystal lad, guileless, unsoiled, dewy, and sparkling as an April raindrop. Ho ho ho.

It never occurred to me not to go; nor did it occur to me to tell Alice Lee Langman I was going—she came home from the dentist to find I had packed and gone. I didn't say good-bye to anybody, just left; I'm the type, and a type by no means rare, who might be your closest friend, a buddy you talked to every day, yet if one day you neglected to make contact, if *you* failed to telephone *me*, then that would be it, we'd never speak again, for *I* would never telephone *you*. I've known lizard-bloods like that and never understood them, even though I was one myself, Just left, yes: sailed at midnight, my heartbeat as raucous as the clanging gongs, the hoarsely hollering smokestacks. I remember watching Manhattan's midnight shine flicker and darken through shivering streamers of confetti—lights I was not to see again for twelve years. And I remember, as I swayed my way down to a tourist-class cabin (having exchanged the first-class passage and pocketed the difference), I remember slipping in a mass of champagne vomit and dislocating my neck. Pity I didn't break it.

When I think of Paris, it seems to me as romantic as a flooded *pissoir*, as tempting as a strangled nude floating in the Seine. Memories of it clear and blue, like scenes emerging between a windshield wiper's languid erasures; and I see myself leaping puddles, for it is always winter and raining, or I see myself seated alone skimming *Time* on the deserted terrace of the Deux Magots, for it is also always a Sunday afternoon in August. I see myself waking in unheated hotel rooms, warped rooms undulating in a Pernod hangover. Across the city, across the bridges, walking down the lonesome vitrine-lined corridor that connects the two entrances of the Ritz hotel, waiting at the Ritz bar for a moneyed American face, cadging drinks there, then later at the Boeuf-sur-le Toit and Brasserie Lipp, then sweating it out until daybreak in some whore-packed nigger-high grope joint blue with Gauloises *bleu;* and awake again in a tilted room swerving with corpse-eyed exuberance. Admittedly, my life was not that of a workaday native; but even the French can't endure France. Or rather, they worship their country but despise their countrymen—unable, as they are, to forgive each other's shared sins: suspicion, stinginess, envy, general meanness. When one has come to loathe a place, it is difficult to recall ever feeling differently. Yet for a wisp of time I held another view. I saw Paris as Denny wanted me to see it, and as he wished he himself still saw it.

(Alice Lee Langman had several nieces, and once the eldest of them, a polite young country girl named Daisy, who had never left Tennessee, visited New York. I groaned when she appeared; it meant my having to move out of Miss Langman's apartment temporarily; worse, I had to cart Daisy around the city, show her the Rockettes, the top of the Empire State Building, the Staten Island Ferry, feed her Nathan's Coney Island hot dogs, baked beans at the Automat, all that junk. Now I remember it with a salty nostalgia; she had a great time, Daisy did, and I had a better one, for it was as though I'd climbed inside her head and were watching and tasting everything from inside that virginal observatory. "Oh," said Daisy, spooning a dish of pistachio ice cream at Rumpelmayer's, "this is crackerjack"; and "Oh," said Daisy, as we joined a Broadway crowd urging a suicide to hurl himself off the ledge of a window in the old Roxy, "oh, this really is cracker-jack.")

Me, I was Daisy in Paris. I spoke no French and never would have if it hadn't been for Denny. He forced me to learn by refusing to speak anything else. Unless we were in bed; however, let me explain that, though he wanted us to share the same bed, his interest in me was romantic but not sexual; nor was he disposed toward anyone else; he said he hadn't had his circle squared in two years, for opium and cocaine had castrated him. We often went to Champs Elysées movies in the afternoon, and at some juncture he always, having begun slightly to sweat, hurried to the men's room and dosed himself with drugs; in the evening he inhaled opium or sipped opium tea, a concoction he brewed by boiling in water the crusts of opium that had accumulated inside his pipe. But he was not a nodder; I never saw him drug-dazed or enfeebled.

Perhaps, at night's end, with approaching daylight edging the drawn bedroom curtains, Denny might lapse a bit and carom off into a curvaceous, opaque outburst. "Tell me, boy, have you ever heard of Father Flanagan's Nigger Queen Kosher Café? Sound familiar? You betcher balls. Even if you never heard of it and maybe think it's some after-hours Harlem dump, even so, you know it by *some* name, and of course you know what it is and where it is. Once I spent a year meditating in a California monastery. Under the super-supervision of His Holiness, the Right Reverend Mr. Gerald Heard. Looking for this . . . Meaningful Thing. This . . . God Thing. *I did try.* No man was ever more naked. Early to bed and early to rise, and prayer, prayer, no hooch, no smokes, I never even jacked off. And all that ever came of that putrid torture was . . . Father Flanagan's Nigger Queen Kosher Café. There it is: right where they throw you off at the end of the line. Just beyond the garbage dump. Watch your step: don't step on the severed head. Now knock. Knock knock. Father Flanagan's voice: 'Who sent ya?' Christ, for Christ's sake, ya dumb mick. Inside . . . it's . . . very . . . relaxing. Because there's not a winner in the crowd. All derelicts, especially those potbellied babies with fat numbered accounts at Crédit Suisse. So you can really unpin your hair, Cinderella. And admit that what we have here is the drop-off. What a relief! Just to throw in the cards, order a Coke, and take a spin around the floor with an old friend like say that *peachy* twelve-year-old Hollywood kid who pulled a Boy Scout knife and robbed me of my very beautiful oval-shaped Cartier watch. The Nigger Queen Kosher Café! The cool green, restful as the grave, rock bottom! That's why I drug: mere dry meditation isn't enough to get me there, keep me there, keep me there, hidden and happy with Father Flanagan and his Outcast of Thousands, him and all the other yids, nigs, spiks, fags, dykes, dope fiends, and commies. Happy to be down there where you belong: Yassah, massuh! Except—the price is too high, I'm killing myself." Then, scrapping the sleazy stand-up-comic tone: "I am, you know. But meeting you has made me change my mind. I wouldn't object to living. Provided you lived with me, Jonesy. It means risking a cure; and it *is* a risk. I've done it once before. At a clinic in Vevey; and every night the mountains collapsed on me, and every morning I wanted to drown myself in Lac Léman. But if I did it, would you? We could go back to the States and buy a filling station. No, no foolin'. I've always wanted to run a filling station. Somewhere in Arizona. Or Nevada. Last Chance for Gas. It would be real quiet, and you could write stories. Basically, I'm pretty healthy. I'm a good cook, too."

Denny offered me drugs, but I refused, and he never insisted, though once he said: "Scared?" Yes, but not of drugs; it was Denny's derelict life that frightened me, and I wanted to emulate him not at all. Strange to remember, but I had preserved the faith: I thought of myself as a serious young man seriously gifted, not an opportunistic layabout, an emotional crook who had drilled Miss Langman till she geysered Guggenheims. I knew I was a bastard but forgave myself because, after all, I was a *born* bastard —a talented one whose sole obligation was to his talent. Despite the nightly upheavals, the brandy heartburns and wine-sour stomachs, I managed every day to turn out five or six pages of a novel; nothing must be allowed to disrupt that, and Denny was in that sense an ominous presence, a heavy passenger—I felt if I didn't free myself that, like Sinbad and the burdensome Old Man, I'd have to cart Denny piggyback the rest of his life. Yet I liked him, at least I didn't want to leave him while he was still uncontrollably narcotized.

So I told him to take the cure. But added: "Let's not make promises. Afterward, you may want to throw yourself at the foot of the cross or end up scrubbing bedpans for Dr. Schweitzer. Or maybe that's *my* destiny." How optimistic I was in those sheltered days!—battling tsetse flies and scraping bedpans with my tongue would be honeyed nirvana compared to the sieges I've since withstood.

It was decided that Denny would travel alone to the clinic in Vevey. We said good-bye at the Gare de Lyon; he was somewhat high on something and looked, with his fresh-colored face—the face of a severe, avengeful angel—twenty years old. His rattling conversation ranged from filling stations to the fact that he had once visited Tibet. At the last Denny said, "If it goes wrong, please do this: destroy everything that's mine. Burn all my clothes. My letters. I wouldn't want Peter having the pleasure."

We agreed not to communicate until Denny had left the clinic; then, presumably, we could meet for a holiday at one of the coastal villages near Naples—Positano or Ravello.

As I had no intention of doing so, or of seeing Denny again if it could be avoided, I moved out of the rue du Bac apartment and into a small room under the eaves of the Hotel Pont Royal. At the time the Pont Royal had a leathery little basement bar that was the favored swill bucket of haute Boheme's fatbacks. Walleyed, pipe-sucking, pasty-hued Sartre and his spinsterish moll, De Beauvoir, were usually propped in a corner like an abandoned pair of ventriloquist's dolls. I often saw Koestler there, never sober; an aggressive runt very free with his fists. And Camus— reedy, diffident in a razory way, a man with crisp brown hair, eyes liquid with life, and a troubled, perpetually listening expression: an approachable person. I knew that he was an editor at Galli- mard, and one afternoon I introduced myself to him as an Ameri- can writer who had published a book of short stories—would he read it, with the thought of Gallimard printing a translation? Later, Camus returned the copy I sent him, with a note saying that his English was insufficient to the task of passing judgment but that he felt I had an ability to create character and tension. "However, I find these stories too abrupt and unrealized. But if you should have other material, please let me see it." Afterward, whenever I encountered Camus at the Pont Royal, and once at a Gallimard garden party that I gate-crashed, he always nodded and smiled encouragement.

Another customer of this bar, whom I met there and who was friendly enough, was the Vicomtesse Marie Laure de Noailles, esteemed poet, a *saloniste* who presided over a drawing room where the ectoplasmic presences of Proust and Reynaldo Hahn were at any moment expected to materialize, the eccentric spouse of a rich sports-minded Marseillais aristocrat, and an affectionate, perhaps undiscriminating, comrade of contemporary Julien Sorels: my slot machine exactly. *Mais alors*—another young American adventurer, Ned Rorem, had emptied that jackpot. Despite her defects—rippling jowls, bee-stung lips, and middle-parted coiffure that eerily duplicated Lautrec's portrait of Oscar Wilde —one could see what Rorem saw in Marie Laure (an elegant roof over his head, someone to promote his melodies in the stratospheres of musical France), but the reverse does not hold. Rorem was from the Midwest, a Quaker queer—which is to say, a queer Quaker—an intolerable combination of brimstone behavior and self-righteous piety. He thought himself Alcibiades reborn, sun-painted, golden, and there were many who seconded his opinion, though I was not among them. For one thing, his skull was criminally contoured: flat-backed, like Dillinger's; and his face, smooth, sweet as cake batter, was a bad blend of the weak and the willful. However, I'm probably being unfair because I envied Rorem, envied him his education, his far more assured reputation as a coming young fellow, and his superior success at playing Living Dildo to Old Hides, as we gigolos call our female check-books. If the subject interests you, you might try reading Ned's own confessional *Paris Diary:* it is well written and cruel as only an outlaw Quaker bent on candor could be. I wonder what Marie Laure thought when she read that book. Of course, she has weath-ered harsher pains than Ned's sniveling revelations could inflict. Her last comrade, or the last known to me, was a hairy Bulgarian painter who killed himself by cutting his wrist and then, wielding a brush and using his severed artery as a palette, covered two walls with a boldly stroked, all-crimson abstract mural.

Indeed, I am indebted to the Pont Royal bar for many acquaint-ances, including the premier American expatriate, Miss Natalie Barney, an heiress of independent mind and morals who had been domiciled in Paris more than sixty years.

For all those decades Miss Barney had lived in the same apart-ment, a suite of surprising rooms off a courtyard in the rue de l'Université. Stained-glass windows and stained-glass skylights— a tribute to Art Nouveau that would have sent good old Boaty into mad-dog delirium: Lalique lamps sculpted as bouquets of milky roses, medieval tables massed with photographs of friends framed in gold and tortoiseshell: Apollinaire, Proust, Gide, Picasso, Cocteau, Radiguet, Colette, Sarah Bernhardt, Stein and

Toklas, Stravinsky, the queens of Spain and Belgium, Nadia Boulanger, Garbo in a snuggly pose with her old buddy Mercedes D'Acosta, and Djuna Barnes, the last a luscious pimento-lipped redhead difficult to recognize as the surly author of *Nightwood* (and latter-day hermit-heroine of Patchin Place). Whatever her calendar age, which must have been eighty and more, Miss Barney, usually attired in virile grey flannel, looked a permanent, pearl-colored fifty. She enjoyed motoring and drove herself about in a canvas-topped emerald Bugatti—around the Bois or out to Versailles on pleasant afternoons. Occasionally, I was asked along, for Miss Barney enjoyed lecturing, and she felt I had much to learn.

Once there was another guest, Miss Stein's widow. The widow wanted to visit an Italian grocery where, she said, it was possible to buy a unique white truffle that came from the hills around Turin. The store was in a distant neighborhood. As our car drove through it, the widow suddenly said: "But aren't we near Romaine's studio?" Miss Barney, while directing at me a disquietingly speculative glance, replied: "Shall we stop there? I have a key."

The widow, a mustachioed spider feeling its feelers, rubbed together her black-gloved hands and said: "Why, it has to be thirty years!"

After climbing six flights of stone stairs inside a dour building saturated with cat urine, that Persian cologne (and Roman, too), we arrived at Romaine's studio—whoever Romaine might be;

neither of my companions explained their friend, but I sensed she had joined the majority and that the studio was being maintained by Miss Barney as a sort of unkempt shrine-museum. A wet afternoon light, oozing through grime-grey skylights, mingled with an immense room's objects: shrouded chairs, a piano with a Spanish shawl, Spanish candelabra with partially burnt candles. Nothing occurred when Miss Barney flicked a light switch.

"Dog take it," she said, suddenly very prairie-American, and lighted up a candelabrum, carrying it with her as she led us around the room to view Romaine Brooks' paintings. There were perhaps seventy of them, all portraits of a flat and ultra realism; the subjects were women, and all of them were dressed identically, each fully outfitted in white tie and tails. You know how you know when you're not going to forget something? I wasn't going to forget this moment, this room, this array of butch-babes, all of whom, to judge from their coifs and cosmetics, were painted between 1917 and 1930.

"Violet," the widow stated as she examined the portrait of a lean bobbed blond with a monocle magnifying an ice-pick eye. "Gertrude liked her. But she seemed to me a cruel girl. I remember she had an owl. She kept it in a cage so small it couldn't move. Simply sat there. With its feathers bursting through the wire. Is Violet still alive?"

Miss Barney nodded. "She has a house in Fiesole. Looks fit as a fiddle. I'm told she's been having the Niehans treatment."

At last we came to a figure I recognized as the widow's lamented mate—depicted here with a Cognac snifter in her left hand and a cheroot in the other, not at all the brown mother-earth monolith Picasso palmed off, but more a Diamond Jim Brady personage, a big-bellied show-off, which one suspects is nearer the truth. "Romaine," said the widow, smoothing her fragile mustache, "Romaine had a certain technique. But she is *not* an artist."

Miss Barney begged to differ. "Romaine," she announced in tones chilled as Alpine slopes, "is a bit limited. *But.* Romaine is a very great artist!"

It was Miss Barney who arranged for me to visit Colette, whom I wanted to meet, not for my usual opportunistic reasons, but because Boaty had introduced me to her work (kindly keep in mind that, intellectually, I am a hitchhiker who gathers his education along highways and under bridges), and I respected her: *My Mother's House* is masterly, incomparable in the artistry of its play upon sensual specifics—taste, scent, touch, sight.

Also, I was curious about this woman; I felt anyone who had lived as broadly as she had, who was as intelligent as she was, must have a few answers. So I was grateful when Miss Barney made it possible for me to have tea with Colette at her apartment in the Palais Royal. "But," warned Miss Barney, speaking on the telephone, "don't tire her by overstaying; she's been ill all winter."

It's true that Colette received me in her bedroom—seated in a golden bed à la Louis Quatorze at his morning levee; but otherwise she seemed as indisposed as a painted Watusi leading a tribal dance. Her *maquillage* was equal to that chore: slanted eyes, lu-

cent as the eyes of a Weimaraner dog, rimmed with kohl; a spare
and clever face powdered clown-pale; her lips, for all her considerable years, were a slippery, shiny, exciting show-girl red; and
her hair was red, or reddish, a rosy blush, a kinky spray. The room
smelled of her perfume (at some point I asked what it was, and
Colette said: "Jicky. The Empress Eugénie always wore it. I like
it because it's an old-fashioned scent with an elegant history, and
because it's witty without being coarse—like the better conversa-
tionalists. Proust wore it. Or so Cocteau tells me. But then he is
not *too* reliable"), of perfume and bowls of fruit and a June breeze
moving voile curtains.

Tea was brought by a maid, who settled the tray on a bed
already burdened with drowsing cats and correspondence, books
and magazines and various bibelots, especially a lot of antique
French crystal paperweights—indeed, many of these precious
objects were displayed on tables and on a fireplace mantel. I had
never seen one before; noticing my interest, Colette selected a
specimen and held its glitter against a lamp's yellow light: "This
one is called The White Rose. As you see, a single white rose
centered in the purest crystal. It was made by the Clichy factory
in 1850. All the great weights were produced between 1840 and
1900 by just three firms—Clichy, Baccarat, and St. Louis. When
I first started buying them, at the flea market and other such casual
places, they were not overly costly, but in the last decades, collect-
ing them has become fashionable, a mania really, and prices are
colossal. To me"—she flashed a globe containing a green lizard

and another with a basket of red cherries inside it—"they are more satisfying than jewelry. Or sculpture. A silent music, these crystal universes. Now," she said, startlingly down to business, "tell me what you expect from life. Fame and fortune aside—those we take for granted." I said, "I don't know what I expect. I know what I'd like. And that is to be a grown-up person."

Colette's painted eyelids lifted and lowered like the slowly beating wings of a great blue eagle. "But that," she said, "is the one thing none of us can ever be: a grown-up person. If you mean a spirit clothed in the sack and ash of wisdom alone? Free of all *mischief*—envy and malice and greed and guilt? Impossible. Voltaire, *even* Voltaire, lived with a child inside him, jealous and angry, a smutty little boy always smelling his fingers. Voltaire carried that child to his grave, as we all will to our own. The pope on his balcony . . . dreaming of a pretty face among the Swiss Guard. And the exquisitely wigged British judge, what is he thinking as he sends a man to the gallows? Of justice and eternity and *mature* matters? Or is he possibly wondering how he can manage election to the Jockey Club? Of course, men have grown-up *moments,* a noble few scattered here and there, and of these, obviously death is the most important. Death certainly sends that smutty little boy scuttling and leaves what's left of us simply an object, lifeless but pure, like The White Rose. Here"—she nudged the flowered crystal toward me—"drop that in your pocket. Keep it as a reminder that to be durable and perfect, to be in fact grown-up, is to be an object, an altar, the figure in a stained-glass window: cherishable stuff. But really, it is so much better to sneeze and feel human."

Once I showed this gift to Kate McCloud, and Kate, who could have worked as an appraiser at Sotheby's, said: "She must have been barking. I mean, whyever did she give it to you? A Clichy weight of that quality is worth . . . oh, quite easily five thousand dollars."

I would as soon not have known its value, not wanting to regard it as a rainy-day reserve. Though I would never sell it, especially now, when I am ass-over-backward down-and-out— because, well, I treasure it as a talisman blessed by a saint of sorts, and the occasions when one does not sacrifice a talisman are at least two: when you have nothing and when you have everything —each is an abyss. Throughout my travels, through hungers and suicidal despairs, a year of hepatitis in a heat-warped, fly-buzzed Calcutta hospital, I have held on to The White Rose. Here at the Y.M.C.A., I have it hidden under my cot; it is tucked inside one of Kate McCloud's old yellow woolen ski socks, which in turn is concealed inside my only luggage, an Air France travel bag (when escaping Southampton, I left pronto, and I doubt that I'll ever again see those Vuitton cases, Battistoni shirts, Lanvin suits, Peal shoes; not that I care to, for the sight would make me strangle on my own vomit).

Just now I fetched it out, The White Rose, and in its winking facets I saw the blue-skied snowfields above St. Moritz and saw Kate McCloud, a russet wraith astride her blond Kneissl skis, streak by in speeding profile, her backward-slanting angle an attitude as elegant and precise as the cool Clichy crystal itself.

It rained night before last; by morning an autumnal flight of dry Canadian air had stopped the next wave, so I went for a walk, and whom should I run into but Woodrow Hamilton!—the man responsible, indirectly anyway, for this last disastrous adventure of mine. Here I am at the Central Park Zoo, empathizing with a zebra, when a disbelieving voice says: "P. B.?" and it was he, the descendant of our twenty-eighth President. "My God, P. B. You look . . ."

I knew how I looked inside my grey skin, my greasy seersucker suit. "Why shouldn't I?"

"Oh. I see. I wondered if you were involved in that. All I know is what I read in the paper. It must be quite a story. Look," he said when I didn't reply, "let's step over to the Pierre and have a drink."

They wouldn't serve me at the Pierre because I wasn't wearing a tie; we wandered over to a Third Avenue saloon, and on the way I decided I wasn't going to discuss Kate McCloud or anything that happened, not out of discretion, but because it was too raw: my spilled guts were still dragging the ground.

Woodrow didn't insist; he may look like a neat nice celluloid square, but really, that's the camouflage that protects the more undulating aspects of his nature. I had last seen him at the Trois Cloches in Cannes, and that was a year ago. He said he had an apartment in Brooklyn Heights and was teaching Greek and Latin at a boys' prep school in Manhattan. "But," he slyly mused, "I have a part-time job. Something that might interest you: if appearances speak, I expect you could use some extra change."

He consulted his wallet and handed me first a hundred-dollar bill: "I earned that just this afternoon, playing ring around the maypole with a Vassar graduate, class of '09"; then a card: "And this is how I met the lady. How I meet them all. Men. Women. Crocodiles. Fuck for fun and profit. At any rate, profit."

The card read: THE SELF SERVICE. PROPRIETOR, MISS VICTORIA SELF. It listed an address on West Forty-second Street and a telephone number with a CIrcle exchange.

"So," said Woodrow, "clean yourself up and go see Miss Self. She'll give you a job."

"I don't think I could handle a job. I'm too strung out. And I'm trying to write again."

Woodrow nibbled the onion in his Gibson. "I wouldn't call it a *job*. Just a few hours a week. After all, what kind of service do you think The Self Service provides?"

"Stud duty, obviously. Dial-a-Dick."

"Ah, you *were* listening—you seemed so fogbound. Stud duty, indeed. But not entirely. It's a co-ed operation. La Self is always ready with anything anywhere anyhow anytime.

"Strange. I would never have pictured you as a stud-for-hire."

"Nor I. But I'm a certain type: good manners, grey suit, horn-rimmed glasses. Believe me, there's plenty of demand. And La

Self specializes in variety. She has everything on her roster from Puerto Rican thugs to rookie cops and stockbrokers."

"Where did she find you?"

"That," said Woodrow, "is too long a tale." He ordered another drink; I declined, for I hadn't tasted liquor since that final incredible gin-crazed session with Kate McCloud, and now just one drink had made me slightly deaf (alcohol first affects my hearing). "I'll only say it was through a guy I knew at Yale. Dick Anderson. He works on Wall Street. A real straight guy, but he hasn't done too well, or well enough to live in Greenwich and have three kids, two of them at Exeter. Last summer I spent a weekend with the Andersons—she's a *real* good gal; Dick and I sat up drinking cold duck, that's this mess made with champagne and sparkling burgundy; boy, it makes me churn to think of it. And Dick said: 'Most of the times I'm disgusted. *Just disgusted.* Goddamn, what a man won't do when he's got two boys in Exeter!' " Woodrow chuckled. "Rather John Cheeverish, no? Respectable but hard-up suburbanite shagging ass to pay his country-club dues and keep his kids in a proper prep."

"No."

"No what?"

"Cheever is too cagey a writer to ever risk a cock-peddling stockbroker. Simply because no one would believe it. His work is always realistic, even when it's preposterous—like *The Enormous Radio* or *The Swimmer.* "

Woodrow was irritated; prudently, I deposited his hundred

dollars inside an inner pocket, where he would have had some trouble retrieving it. "If it's true, and it is, why would anyone not believe it?"

"Because something is true doesn't mean that it's convincing, either in life or in art. Think of Proust. Would *Remembrance* have the ring that it does if he had made it historically literal, if he hadn't transposed sexes, altered events and identities? If he had been absolutely factual, it would have been less believable, but" —this was a thought I'd often had—"it might have been better. Less acceptable, but better." I decided on another drink, after all. "That's the question: is truth an illusion, or is illusion truth, or are they essentially the same? Myself, I don't care what anybody says about me as long as it isn't true."

"Maybe you ought to skip that other drink."

"You think I'm drunk?"

"Well, you're rambling."

"I'm relaxed, that's all."

Woodrow kindly said: "So you've started writing again. Novel?"

"A report. An account. Yes, I'll *call* it a novel. If I ever finish it. Of course, I never do finish anything."

"Have you a title?" Oh, Woodrow was right there with all the garden-party queries.

"Answered Prayers."

Woodrow frowned. "I've heard that before."

"Not unless you were one of the three hundred schlunks who

bought my first and only published work. That, too, was called *Answered Prayers.* For no particular reason. This time I have a reason."

"*Answered Prayers.* A quote, I suppose."

"St. Teresa. I never looked it up myself, so I don't know exactly what she said, but it was something like 'More tears are shed over answered prayers than unanswered ones.' "

Woodrow said: "I see a light flickering. This book—it's about Kate McCloud, *and* gang."

"I wouldn't say it's *about* them—though they're in it."

"Then what is it about?"

"Truth as illusion."

"And illusion as truth?"

"The first. The second is another proposition."

Woodrow asked how so, but the whiskey was at work and I felt too deaf to tell him; but what I *would* have said was: as truth is nonexistent, it can never be anything but illusion—but illusion, the by-product of revealing artifice, can reach the summits nearer the unobtainable peak of Perfect Truth. For example, female impersonators. The impersonator is in fact a man (truth), until he re-creates himself as a woman (illusion)—and of the two, the illusion is the truer.

Around five that afternoon, as offices were emptying, I found myself trawling along Forty-second Street, looking for the address listed on Miss Self's card. The establishment turned out to

be located above a ground-floor pornographic emporium, one of
those dumps plastered with poster portraits of dangling dongs and
split beavers. As I approached it, an exiting customer, someone of
respectable and unimportant appearance, dropped a package,
which opened, scattering across the pavement several dozen
black-and-white glossies—nothing extra, the usual sixty-niners
and marshmallow gals getting a three-way ride; still, a number of
pedestrians paused to stare as the owner knelt to recover his
property. Pornography, in my opinion, has been much misunder-
stood, for it doesn't develop sex fiends and send them roaming
alleyways—it is an anodyne for the sexually oppressed and unre-
quited, for what is the aim of pornography if not to stimulate
masturbation? And surely masturbation is the pleasanter alternative for men "on the muscle," as they say in horse-breeding circles.

A Puerto Rican pimp stood sneering at the stooped man
("What you want with that when I got nice live *puta?*"), but I
felt sorry for him: he looked to me like some youngish lonely
minister who had embezzled the whole of last Sunday's collection plate to buy those jack-off snaps; so I decided to help him
pick them up—but the instant I began, he struck me across the
face: a karate chop that felt as if it must have shattered a cheek-
bone.

"Beat it," he snarled. I said: "Jesus, I wanted to help you." And
he said: "Beat it. Before I bust you good." His face had flushed
a red so bright it pained my eyes, and then I realized it wasn't

exclusively the color of rage but of shame as well—I thought he'd thought I meant to steal his pictures, when really what had infuriated him was the pity implicit in my proffered assistance.

Though Miss Self is a most successful businesswoman, she certainly doesn't squander on display. Her offices are four flights up in an elevatorless building. THE SELF SERVICE: a frosted-glass door with that inscription. But I hesitated (really, did I want to do this? Well, there wasn't anything I'd *rather* do, at least to make money). I combed my hair, creased the trousers of a just-bought fifty-dollar Robert Hall herringbone two-pants special, rang, and walked in.

The outer office was unfurnished except for a bench, a desk, and two young gentlemen, one of them a secretary-receptionist seated behind the desk and the other a beautiful mulatto wearing a *very* contemporary dark blue silk suit; neither one chose to notice me.

". . . so after that," the mulatto was saying, "I stayed a week with Spencer in San Diego. Spencer! He is ooooee some *rocket*, wow. One night we were parachuting along the San Diego Freeway, and Spencer picked up this spade marine, a real country-boy piece of smoked Alabama beef, so Spencer was like going after it in the back seat, and afterward the guy says: 'I sho can see what I git outta it. It feel good. But what I sho can't see is what you fellas git outta it.' And Spencer tells him: 'Ah, man. It's deelicious. Jes pussy on a stick.' "

51

The secretary languidly turned upon me a disapproving pair of wintergreen eyes. A blond, and how!—his skin had the golden oleo gleam that comes from long Cherry Grove weekends. Yet, overall, he seemed decidedly moldy—a sort of suntanned Uriah Heep. "Yes?" he inquired in a voice that crawled coolly through the air like an exhalation of mentholated smoke.

I told him I wanted to see Miss Self. He asked my purpose, and I said I had been recommended by Woodrow Hamilton. He said: "You will have to fill out our form. Are you applying as a client? Or as a prospective employee?"

"Employee."

"Mmmmm," mused Black Beauty, "that's too bad. I wouldn't have minded scrambling your eggs, daddy." And the secretary, prissily pissed-off, said: "Okay, Lester. Shove your sore ass off sister's desk and hustle it down to the Americana. You've got a five-thirty. Room 507."

When I had completed the questionnaire, which asked nothing beyond the customary Age? Address? Occupation? Marital Status?, Dracula's daughter evaporated with it into an inner office—and while he was gone, this girl ambled in, an overweight but damned attractive girl, a young *boule de suif* with a pink creamy round face and a fat pair of boobs squirming inside the bodice of a summery pink dress.

She cuddled down next to me and tucked a cigarette between her lips. "How about it?" I explained if it was a match she wanted, I couldn't help her as I'd stopped smoking, and she said: "So have

I. This is just a prop. I meant how about it, where's Butch? Butch!" she cried, rising to engulf the returning secretary.

"Maggie!"

"Butch!"

"Maggie!" Then, coming to his senses: "You bitch. Five days! Where have you been?"

"Didja miss Maggie?"

"Fuck *me*. What do *I* count? But that old guy from Seattle. Oy vey, the hell he raised when you stood him up Thursday night."

"I'm sorry, Butch. Gee."

"But where *have* you been, Maggie? I went to your hotel twice. I called a hundred times. You might have checked in."

"I know. But see . . . I got married."

"Married? Maggie!"

"Please, Butch. It's nothing serious. It won't *interfere.*"

"I can't imagine what Miss Self will say." And at last he remembered me. "Oh, yes," this secretary said, as if flicking lint off a sleeve, "Miss Self will see you now, Mr. Jones. Miss Self," he announced, opening a door for me, "this is Mr. Jones."

She looked like Marianne Moore; a stouter, Teutonized Miss Moore. Grey hausfrau braids pinioned her narrow skull; she wore no makeup, and her suit, one might say uniform, was of prison-matron blue serge—a lady altogether as lacking in luxury as were her premises. *Except* . . . on her wrist I noticed a gold oval-shaped watch with Roman numerals. Kate McCloud had one just like it; it had been given her by John F. Kennedy, and it came from

Cartier in London, where it had cost twelve hundred dollars.

"Sit down, please." Her voice was rather teacup-timid, but her cobalt eyes had the 20/20 steeliness of a gangland hit man. She glanced at the watch that was so out of keeping with her inelegant texture. "Will you join me? It's well after five." And she extracted from a desk drawer two shot glasses and a bottle of tequila, something I'd never tasted and didn't expect to like. "You'll like it," she said. "It's got balls. My third husband was Mexican. Now tell me," she said, tapping my application form, "have you ever done this work before? Professionally?"

Interesting question; I thought about it. "I wouldn't say *professionally*. But I've done it for . . . profit."

"That's professional enough. Kicks!" she said and hooked down a neat jigger of tequila. She grimaced. Shuddered. *"Buenos Dios,* that's hairy. *Hairy.* Go on," she said. "Knock it back. You'll like it."

It tasted to me like perfumed benzine.

"Now," she said, "I'm going to roll you some clean dice, Jones. Middle-aged men account for ninety percent of our clientele, and half our trade is offbeat stuff one way and another. So if you want to register here strictly as a straight stud, forget it. Are you with me?"

"All the way."

She winked and poured herself another shot. "Tell me, Jones. Is there anything you won't do?"

"I won't catch. I'll pitch. But I won't catch."

"Ah, so?" She *was* German; it was only the souvenir of an accent, like a scent of cologne lingering on an antique handkerchief. "Is this a moral prejudice?"

"Not really. Hemorrhoids."

"How about S. and M.? F.F.?"

"The whole bit?"

"Yes, dear. Whips. Chains. Cigarettes. F.F. That sort of thing."

"I'm afraid not."

"Ah, so? And is *this* a moral prejudice?"

"I don't believe in cruelty. Even when it gives someone else pleasure."

"Then you have never been cruel?"

"I didn't say that."

"Stand up," she said. "Take off your jacket. Turn around. Again. More slowly. Too bad you aren't a bit taller. But you've got a good figure. A nice flat stomach. How well hung are you?"

"I've never had any complaints."

"Perhaps our audience is more demanding. You see, that's the one question they always ask: how big is his joint?"

"Want to see it?" I said, toying with my super-special Robert Hall fly.

"There is no reason to be crude, Mr. Jones. You will learn that although I am someone who speaks directly, I am not a *crude* person. Now sit down," she said, refilling both our tequila glasses. "So far I have been the inquisitor. What would you like to know?"

What I wanted to know was her life story; few people have made me so immediately curious. Was she perhaps a Hitler refugee, a veteran of Hamburg's Reeperbahn, who had emigrated to Mexico before the war? And it crossed my mind that possibly she was not the power behind this operation but, like most American brothel keepers and sex-café padrones, a front for Mafioso entrepreneurs.

"Cat got your tongue? Well, I'm sure you will want to understand our financial agreement. The standard fee for an hour's booking is fifty dollars, which we will split between us, though you may keep any tips the client gives you. Of course, the fee varies; there will be occasions when you will make a great deal more. And there are bonuses available for every acceptable client or employee you recruit. Now," she said, aiming her eyes at me like a pair of gun barrels, "there are a number of rules by which you must abide. There will be no drugging or excessive drinking. Under no circumstances will you ever deal directly with a client —all bookings must be made through the service. And at no time may an employee associate socially with a client. Any attempt at negotiating a private deal with a client means instant dismissal. Any attempt at blackmailing or in any way embarrassing a client will result in very severe retribution—by which I don't mean mere dismissal from the service."

So: those dark Sicilian spiders are indeed the weavers of this web.

"Have I made myself understood?"

"Utterly."

The secretary intruded. "Mr. Wallace calling. Very urgent. I think he's smashed."

"We are not interested in your opinions, Butch. Just put the gentleman on the line." Presently she lifted a receiver, one of several on her desk. "Miss Self here. How are you, sir? I thought you were in Rome. Well, I read it in the *Times*. That you were in Rome and had had an audience with the pope. Oh, I'm sure you're right: *quel* camp! Yes, I hear you perfectly. I see. I see." She scribbled on a note pad, and I could read what she wrote because one of my gifts is to read upside down: *Wallace Suite 713 Hotel Plaza*. "I'm sorry, but Gumbo isn't with us anymore. These black boys, they're so unreliable. However, we'll have someone there shortly. Not at all. Thank you."

Then she looked at me for quite a long time. "Mr. Wallace is a highly valued client." Once more a prolonged stare. "Wallace isn't his name, of course. We use pseudonyms for all our clients. Employees as well. Your name is Jones. We'll call you Smith."

She tore off the sheet of note pad, rolled it into a pellet, and tossed it at me. "I think you can handle this. It's not really a . . . physical situation. It's more a . . . nursing problem."

I rang Mr. Wallace on one of those sleazy gold housephones in the Plaza lobby. A dog answered—there was the sound of a crashing receiver, followed by a hounds-of-hell barking. "Heh heh, that's just mah dawg," a corn-pone voice explained. "Every time the phone rings, he grabs it. You the fellow from the service? Well, skedaddle on up here."

When the client opened the door, his dog bolted into the corridor and hurled himself at me like a New York Giants fullback. It was a black and brindle English bulldog—two feet high, maybe three feet wide; he had to weigh a hundred pounds, and the force of his attack hurricaned me against the wall. I hollered pretty good; the owner laughed: "Don't be scared. Old Bill, he's just affectionate." I'll say. The horny bastard was riding my leg like a doped stallion. "Bill, you cut that out," Bill's master commanded in a voice jingling with gin-slurred giggles. "I mean it, Bill. Quit that." At last he attached a leash to the sex fiend's collar and hauled him off me, saying: "Poor Bill. I've just been in no condition to walk him. Not for two days. That's one reason I called the service. The first thing I want you to do is to take Bill over to the park."

Bill behaved until we reached the park.

En route, I considered Mr. Wallace: a chunky, paunchy booze-puffed runt with a play mustache glued above laconic lips. Time had interred his looks, for he used to be reasonably presentable; nevertheless, I had recognized him immediately, even though I'd seen him only once before, and that some ten years earlier. But I remembered that former glimpse of him distinctly, for at that time he was the most acclaimed American playwright, and in my opinion the best; also, the curious *mise-en-scène* contributed to my memory: it was after midnight in Paris in the bar of the Boeuf-sur-le-Toit, where he was sitting at a pink-clothed table with three men, two of them expensive tarts, Corsican pirates in British flannel, and the third none other than Sumner Welles—fans of *Confidential* will remember the patrician Mr. Welles, former Undersecretary of State, great and good friend of the Brotherhood of Sleeping Car Porters. It made rather a tableau, one especially *vivant,* when His Excellency, pickled as brandied peaches, began nibbling those Corsican ears.

Autumn strollers eased along the park's evening paths. A Nipponese couple paused to spend affection on Bill; in a way they went out of their minds, tugging his twisted tail, hugging him— I could understand it because Bill, with his indented face and Quasimodo legs, his intricately contorted physique, was an object as appealing to an Oriental sense of the aesthetic as bonsai trees and dwarf deer and goldfish bred to weigh five pounds. However, I myself am not Oriental, and when Bill, after luring me onto the grass and under a tree, suddenly again sexually attacked me, I was not appreciative.

Being no match for so determined a rapist, it was expedient just to lie back on the grass and let him have his way—even encourage him: That's it, baby. Give it to me good. Get your rocks off." We had an audience—human faces bobbed in the distance beyond my frolicking lover's bulging passion-doped eyes. Some woman harshly said: "You filthy degenerate! Stop abusing that animal! Why doesn't anybody call a policeman?" Another woman said: "Albert, I want to go back to Utica. Tonight." With slobbering gasps, Bill crossed his chest.

My drenched Robert Hall trousers were not Bill's only offense against me ere the eve was o'er. When I returned him to the Plaza and entered the foyer of the suite, I stepped into a big pile of wet shit, Bill's shit, and skidded and fell flat on my face—into a *second* pile of shit. All I said to Mr. Wallace was: "Do you mind if I take a shower?" He said: "I always insist on that."

However, as Miss Self had suggested, Mr. Wallace, like Denny Fouts, was more conversationalist than sensualist. "You're a good kid," he advised me. "Oh, I know you're no kid. I'm not that drunk. I can see you got mileage on you. But never mind, you're a good kid; it's in your eyes. Wounded eyes. Injured and insulted. Read Dostoevski? Well, I guess that's not your racket. But you're one of his people. Insulted and injured. Me too; that's why I feel safe with you." He rolled his eyes around the lamplit bedroom like an espionage agent; the room looked as if a Kansas twister had just gone through—messy laundry everywhere, dog shit all over the place, and drying puddles of dog piss marking the rugs. Bill was asleep at the foot of the bed, his snores exuding postcoital melancholy. At least he allowed his master and his master's guest to share the bed a bit, the guest naked but the master fully dressed, down to black shoes and a vest with pencils in the pocket and a pair of horn-rimmed glasses. In one hand Mr. Wallace gripped a toothpaste glass brimming with undiluted Scotch and in the other a cigar that kept accumulating trembling lengths of ash. Occasionally he reached to stroke me, and once the hot ash singed my navel; I thought it was on purpose, but decided perhaps not.

"As safe as a hunted man can feel. A man with murderers on his trail. I'm liable to die very suddenly. And if I do, it won't be a natural death. They'll try to make it look like heart failure. Or an accident. But promise me you won't believe that. Promise me you'll write a letter to the *Times* and tell them it was murder."

With drunks and madmen, always be logical. "But if you think you're in danger, why don't you call the cops?"

He said: "I'm no squealer"; then he added: "I'm a dying man, anyway. Dying of cancer."

"What kind of cancer is it?"

"Blood. Throat. Lungs. Tongue. Stomach. Brain. Asshole." Alcoholics really despise the taste of alcohol; he shivered as he bolted half the Scotch in his glass. "It all started seven years ago when the critics turned on me. Every writer has his tricks, and sooner or later the critics catch them. That's all right; they love you as long as they've got you identified. My mistake was I got sick of my old tricks and learned some new ones. Critics won't put up with that; they hate versatility—they don't like to see a writer grow or change in any way. So that's when the cancer came. When the critics started saying the old tricks were 'the stuff of pure poetic power' and the new tricks were 'shabby pretensions.' Six failures in a row, four on Broadway and two off. They're killing me out of envy and ignorance. And without shame or remorse. What do they care that cancer's eating my brain!" Then, quite complacently, he said: "You don't believe me, do you?"

"I can't believe in seven years of galloping cancer. That's impossible."

"I'm a dying man. But you don't believe it. You don't believe I have cancer at all. You think it's all a problem for the shrinker." No, what I thought was: here's a dumpy little guy with a dramatic mind who, like one of his own adrift heroines, seeks attention and sympathy by serving up half-believed lies to total strangers. Strangers because he has no friends, and he has no friends because the only people he pities are his own characters and himself—everyone else is an audience. "But for your information, I've been to a shrink. I spent sixty bucks an hour five days a week for two years. All the bastard did was interfere in my personal affairs."

"Isn't that what they're paid to do? Interfere in one's personal affairs?"

"Don't get smart with me, old buddy. This is no joke. Dr. Kewie ruined my life. He convinced me I wasn't a queer and that I didn't love Fred. He told me I was finished as a writer unless I got rid of Fred. But the truth was Fred was the only good thing in my life. Maybe I didn't love *him*. But he loved *me*. He held my life together. He wasn't the phony Kewie said he was. Kewie said: Fred doesn't love you, he loves your money. The one who loves money is Kewie. Well, I wouldn't leave Fred, so Kewie calls him secretly and tells him I'm going to die of drink if he doesn't clear out. Fred packs and disappears, and I can't understand it until Dr. Kewie, very proud of himself, confesses what he's done. And I told him: You see, Fred believed you and because he loved me so much he sacrificed himself. But I was wrong about that. Because when we found Fred, and I hired Pinkertons who found him in Puerto Rico, Fred said all he wanted to do was bust me in the nose. He thought *I* was the one who had put Kewie up to calling him, that it was all a plot on my part. Still, we made up. A lot of good it did. Fred was operated on at Memorial Hospital June seventeenth, and he died the fourth of July. He was only thirty-six years old. But he wasn't pretending; he really had cancer. And that's what comes of shrinkers interfering in your private life. Look at the mess! Imagine having to hire whores to walk Bill."

"I'm not a whore." Though I don't know why I bothered protesting: I am a whore and always have been.

He grunted sarcastically; like all maudlin men, he was cold-hearted. "How about it?" he said, blowing the ash off his cigar. "Roll over and spread those cheeks."

"Sorry, but I don't catch. Pitch, yes. Catch, no."

"Ohhh," he said, his way-down-yonder voice mushy as sweet-potato pie, "I don't want to cornhole you, old buddy. I just want to put out my cigar."

Boy, did I beat it out of there!—hustled my clothes into the bathroom and bolted the door. While dressing, I could hear Mr. Wallace chuckling to himself. "Old buddy?" he said. "You didn't think I meant it, did you, old buddy? I don't know. Nobody's got a sense of humor anymore." But when I came out, he was snoring slightly, a soft accompaniment to Bill's robust racket. The cigar still burned between his fingers: probably someday when no one is there to save him, this will be the way Mr. Wallace will go.

Here at the Y a sixty-year-old blind man sleeps in the cell next to mine. He is a masseur and has been employed for several months by the gym downstairs. His name is Bob, and he is a big-bellied guy who smells of baby oil and Sloan's Liniment. Once I mentioned to him that I had worked as a masseur, and he said he'd like to see what kind of masseur I was, so we traded techniques, and while he was rubbing me with his thick sensitive blind-man's hands, he told me a bit about himself. He said he'd been a bachelor until he was fifty, when he married a San Diego waitress. "Helen. She described herself as a gorgeous blond piece-ass thirty-one years old, a divor-cée, but I don't guess she could have been much, else why would she have married me? She had a good figure, though, and with these hands I could get her plenty hot. Well, we bought a Ford pickup and a little aluminum house trailer and moved to Cathedral City—that's in the California desert near Palm Springs. I figured I could get work at one of the clubs in Palm Springs, and I did. It's a great place November to June, best climate in the world, hot in the daytime and cold at night, but Jesus the summers, it could go to a hundred twenty, thirty, and it wasn't dry heat like you'd expect, not since they built them million swimming pools out there: them pools made the desert *humid,* and humid at a hundred twenty ain't for white men. Or women.

"Helen suffered terrible, but there was nothing to do—I never could save enough in the winter to get us away from there in the summer. We fried alive in our little aluminum trailer. Just sat there, Helen watching TV and coming to hate me. Maybe she'd always hated me; or our life; or *her* life. But since she was a quiet woman and we never quarreled much, I didn't know how she felt till last April. That's when I had to quit work and go into the hospital for an operation. Varicose veins in my legs. I didn't have the money, but it was a matter of life and death. The doctor said otherwise I could have an embolism any minute. It was three days after the operation before Helen come to see me. She doesn't say how are you or kiss me or nothing. What she said was: 'I don't want anything, Bob. I left a suitcase downstairs with your clothes. All I'm taking is the truck and the trailer.' I ask her what she's talking about, and she says: 'I'm sorry, Bob. But I've got to move on.' I was scared; I began to cry—I begged her, I said: 'Helen, please, woman, I'm blind and now I'm lame and I'm sixty years old—you can't leave me like this without a home and nowhere to turn.' Know what she said? 'When you've got nowhere to turn, turn on the gas.' And those were the last words she ever spoke to me. When I got out of the hospital, I had fourteen dollars and seventy-eight cents, but I wanted to put as much space between me and there as ever I could, so I hit out for New York, hitchhiking. Helen, wherever she is, I hope she's happier. I don't hold anything against her, though I think she treated me extra hard. That was a tough deal, an old blind man and half lame, hitchhiking all the way across America."

A helpless man waiting in the dark by the side of an unknown road: that's how Denny Fouts must have felt, for I had been as heartless to him as Helen had been to Bob.

Denny had sent me two messages from the Vevey clinic. The script of the first was all but unintelligible: "Difficult to write as I cannot control my hands. Father Flanagan, renowned proprietor of Father Flanagan's Nigger Queen Kosher Café, has given me my check and shown me the door. Merci Dieu pour toi. Otherwise I would feel very alone." Six weeks later I received a firmly written card: "Please telephone me at Vevey 46 27 14."

I placed the call from the bar of the Pont Royal; I remember, as I waited for Denny's voice, watching Arthur Koestler methodically abuse a woman who was seated with him at a table—someone said she was his girl friend; she was crying but did nothing to protect herself from his insults. It is intolerable to see a man weep or a woman bullied, but no one intervened, and the bartenders and waiters pretended not to notice.

Then Denny's voice descended from alpine altitudes—he sounded as if his lungs were filled with brilliant air; he said it had been rough-going, but he was ready now to leave the clinic, and could I meet him Tuesday in Rome, where Prince Ruspoli ("Dado") had lent him an apartment. I am cowardly—in the frivolous sense and also the most serious; I can never be more than moderately truthful about my feelings toward another person, and I will say yes when I mean no. I told Denny I would meet

66

him in Rome, for how could I say I never meant to see him again because he scared me? It wasn't the drugs and chaos but the funereal halo of waste and failure that hovered above him: the shadow of such failure seemed somehow to threaten my own impending triumph.

So I went to Italy, but to Venice, not Rome, and it wasn't until early winter, when I was alone one night in Harry's Bar, that I learned that Denny had died in Rome a few days after I was supposed to have joined him. Mimi told me. Mimi was an Egyptian fatter than Farouk, a drug smuggler who shuttled between Cairo and Paris; Denny was devoted to Mimi, or at least devoted to the narcotics Mimi supplied, but I scarcely knew him and was surprised when, seeing me in Harry's, Mimi waddled over and kissed my cheek with his drooling raspberry lips and said: "I have to laugh. Whenever I think about Denny, I got to laugh. *He* would have laughed. To die like that! It could only have happened to Denny." Mimi raised his plucked eyebrows. "Ah. You didn't know? It was the cure. If he had stayed on dope, he would have lived another twenty years. But the cure killed him. He was sitting on the toilet taking a crap when his heart gave out." According to Mimi, Denny was buried in the Protestant cemetery near Rome—but the following spring when I searched there for his grave, I couldn't find it.

For many years I was very partial to Venice, and I have lived there in all seasons, preferring late autumn and winter when sea mist drifts through the piazzas and the silvery rustle of gondola bells shivers the veiled canals. I spent the whole of my first European winter there, living in an unheated little apartment on the top floor of a Grand Canal palazzo. I've never known such cold; there were moments when surgeons could have amputated my arms and legs without my feeling the slightest pain. Still, I wasn't unhappy, because I was convinced my work in progress, *Sleepless Millions,* was a masterpiece. Now I know it for what it was—a dog's dinner of surrealist prose saucing a Vicki Baum recipe. Though I blush to admit it, but just for the record, it was about a dozen or so Americans (a divorcing couple, a fourteen-year-old girl in a motel room with a young and rich and handsome male voyeur, a masturbating marine general, etc.) whose lives were linked together only by the circumstance that they were watching a late-late movie on television.

I worked on the book every day from nine in the morning until three in the afternoon, and at three, no matter what the weather, I went hiking through the Venetian maze until it was nightfall and time to hit Harry's Bar, blow in out of the cold and into the hearth-fire cheer of Mr. Cipriani's microscopic fine-food-and-drink palace. Harry's in winter is a different kind of madhouse from what it is the rest of the year—just as crowded, but at Christmas the premises belong not to the English and Americans but to an eccentric local aristocracy, pale foppish young counts and creaking principessas, citizens who wouldn't put a foot in the place until after October, when the last couple from Ohio has departed. Every night I spent nine or ten dollars in Harry's—on martinis and shrimp sandwiches and heaping bowls of green noo-dles with sauce Bolognese. Though my Italian has never amounted to much, I made a lot of friends and could tell you about many a wild time (but, as an old New Orleans acquaintance of mine used to say: "Baby, don't let me commence!").

The only Americans I remember meeting that winter were Peggy Guggenheim and George Arvin, the latter an American painter, very gifted, who looked like a blond crew-cut basketball coach; he was in love with a gondolier and had for years lived in Venice with the gondolier and the gondolier's wife and children (somehow this arrangement finally ended, and when it did Arvin entered an Italian monastery, where in time he became, so I'm told, a brother of the order).

Remember my wife, Hulga? If it hadn't been for Hulga, the fact we were legally chained, I might have married the Guggenheim woman, even though she was maybe thirty years my senior, maybe more. And if I had, it wouldn't have been because she tickled me—despite her habit of rattling her false teeth and even though she did rather look like a long-haired Bert Lahr. It was pleasant to spend a Venetian winter's evening in the compact white Palazzo dei Leoni, where she lived with eleven Tibetan terriers and a Scottish butler who was always bolting off to Lon-don to meet his lover, a circumstance his employer did not com-plain about because she was snobbish and the lover was said to be

Prince Philip's valet; pleasant to drink the lady's good red wine and listen while she remembered aloud her marriages and affairs —it astonished me to hear, situated inside that gigolo-ish brigade, the name Samuel Beckett. Hard to conceive of an odder coupling, this rich and worldly Jewess and the monkish author of *Molloy* and *Waiting for Godot*. It makes one *wonder* about Beckett . . . and his pretentious aloofness, austerity. Because impoverished, unpublished scribes, which is what Beckett was at the time of the liaison, do not take as mistresses homely American copper heiresses without having something more than love in mind. Myself, my admiration for her notwithstanding, I guess I would have been pretty interested in her swag anyway, but the only reason I didn't run true to form by trying to get some of it away from her was that conceit had turned me into a plain damn fool; everything was to be mine the day *Sleepless Millions* saw print.

Except that it never did.

In March, when I finished the manuscript, I sent a copy to my agent, Margo Diamond, a pockmarked muffdiver who had been persuaded to handle me by another of her clients, my old discard Alice Lee Langman. Margo replied that she had submitted the novel to the publisher of my first book, *Answered Prayers*. "However," she wrote me, "I have done this only as a courtesy, and if they turn it down, I'm afraid you will have to find another agent, as I feel it is not in your own best interest, or mine, for me to continue representing you. I will admit that your conduct toward Miss Langman, the extraordinary manner in which you repaid her generosity, has influenced my opinion. Still, I would not let that deter me if I felt you had gifts that must at all costs be encouraged. But I do not and never have. You are not an artist —and if you are not an artist, then you must at least show promise of becoming a truly skilled professional writer. But there is a lack of discipline, a consistent unevenness, that suggests professionalism is beyond you. Why not, while you are still young, consider another career?"

Slit-slavering bitch! Boy (I thought), would she be sorry! And even when I arrived in Paris and found at the American Express a letter from the publisher rejecting the book ("Regrettably, we feel we would be doing you a disservice to sponsor your debut as a novelist with so contrived a work as *Sleepless Millions . . .* ") and asking what I wished them to do with the manuscript, even then my faith never faltered: I just supposed that, owing to my having abandoned Miss Langman, her friends were now making me the victim of a literary lynching.

I had fourteen thousand dollars left from my various swindles and savings, and I did not want to return stateside. But there seemed no alternative, not if I wanted to see *Sleepless Millions* published: it would be impossible to market the book from such a distance and without an agent. An honest and competent agent is more difficult to secure than a reputable publisher. Margo Diamond was among the best; she was as chummy with the staffs of snobrags, like *The New York Review of Books,* as she was with the editors of *Playboy.* Maybe she did think I was untalented, but really it was jealousy—because what that fishhound had always wanted to do was T the V with La Langman herself. However, the prospect of going back to New York made my stomach lurch and dip with roller-coaster aggressiveness. It seemed to me I could never reenter that city, where I now had no friends and many enemies, unless preceded by marching bands and all the confetti of success. To return droop-tailed and toting an unsold novel required someone with either lesser or greater character than I had.

Among the planet's most pathetic tribes, sadder than a huddle of homeless Eskimos starving through a winter night seven months long, are those Americans who elect, out of vanity, or for supposedly aesthetic reasons, or because of sexual or financial problems, to make a career of expatriation. The fact of surviving abroad year upon year, of trailing spring from Taroudant in January to Taormina to Athens to Paris in June, is, of itself, the justification for superior postures and a sense of exceptional achievement. Indeed, it *is* an achievement if you have little money or, like most of the American remittance men, "just enough to live on." If you're young enough, it's okay for a couple of years—but those who pursue it after age twenty-five, thirty at the limit, learn that what seemed paradise is mere scenery, a curtain that, lifting, reveals pitchforks and fire.

Yet gradually I was absorbed into this squalid caravan, though it was some while before I recognized what had happened. As summer started and I decided not to return but to try to market my book by mailing it around to different publishers, my head-splitting days began with several Pernods on the terrace of the Deux Magots; after that, I stepped across the boulevard into Brasserie Lipp for choucroute and beer, lots of beer, followed by a siesta in my nice little river-view room in the Hotel Quai Voltaire. The real drinking began around six, when I took a taxi to the Ritz, where I spent the early evening hours cadging martinis at the bar; if I didn't make a connection there, solicit an invitation to dinner from some closet queen or occasionally from two ladies traveling together or perhaps from a naïve American couple, then usually I didn't eat. My guess would be that, in a nutritional sense, I consumed less than five hundred calories a day. But booze, particularly the sickening balloons of Calvados I emptied every night in writhing Senegalese cabarets and bent-type bars, like Le Fiacre and Mon Jardin and Madame Arthur's and Boeuf-sur-le-Toit, kept me looking, for all my disintegrating interior, well-filled and sturdy. But despite the waterfall hangovers and constant cascading nausea, I was under the strange impression that I was having a damn good time, the kind of educational experience necessary to an artist—and it is true that a number of those persons whom I encountered in my carousings cut through the Calvados mists to leave scrawled across my mind permanent signatures.

Which brings us to Kate McCloud. Kate! McCloud! My love, my anguish, my Götterdämmerung, my very own *Death in Venice:* inevitable, perilous as the asp at Cleopatra's breast.

It was late winter in Paris; I had returned there after spending several unsober months in Tangier, most of them as a habitué of Jay Hazlewood's Le Parade, a swanky little joint operated by a kind and gangling Georgia guy who had made a moderate fortune from dispensing proper martinis and jumbo hamburgers to homesick Americans; he also, for the favored of his foreign clientele, served up the asses of Arab lads and lassies—without charge of course, just a courtesy of the house.

One night at the bar at Parade, I met someone who was to influence future events immensely. He had slicked-down blond hair parted in the middle, like a hair-tonic ad published in the twenties; he was trim and freckled and fresh-colored; he had a good smile and healthy teeth, if a few too many of them. He had a pocketful of kitchen matches that he kept lighting with his thumbnail. He was about forty, an American, but with one of those off-center accents that happen to people who are used to speaking a number of languages: it's not an affectation but rather more like an indefinable speech defect. He bought me a couple of drinks, we rolled some dice; later I asked Jay Hazlewood about him.

"Nobody," said Jay in his deceptive red-clay drawl. "His name is Aces Nelson."

"But what does he do?"

Jay said, and said it *so* solemnly: "He's a friend of the rich."

"And that's all?"

"All? Shit!" said Jay Hazlewood. "Being a friend of the rich, making a living out of it, one day of that is harder than a month's worth of twenty niggers working on a chain gang."

"But *how* does he make a living out of it?"

Hazlewood widened one eye, squinted the other—a Dixie horse trader—but I wasn't joshing him: I really didn't understand.

"Look," he said, "there are a lot of pilot fish like Aces Nelson. There's nothing special about him. Except that he's a little cuter than most of them. Aces is okay. Comparatively. He hits Tangier two, three times a year, always on someone's yacht; he spends every summer moving from one yacht to another—the *Gaviota*, the *Siesta*, the *Christina*, the *Sister Anne*, the *Creole*, you name it. The rest of the year he's up in the Alps—St. Moritz or Gstaad. Or the West Indies. Antigua. Lyford Cay. With stopovers in Paris, New York, Beverly Hills, Grosse Pointe. But wherever he is, he's always doing the same thing. He's sweating for his supper. By playing games—from lunch till lights-out. Bridge. Gin. Cut-throat. Old Maid, Backgammon. Beaming. Flashing his capped teeth. Keeping the Geritols happy in their oceangoing salons. That's how he makes his walking-around money. The rest of it comes from pumping broads of various ages and hungers—rich quim with husbands that don't give a damn who does them as long as they don't have to."

Jay Hazlewood never smoked: a true son of the Georgia hills, he chewed plug tobacco. Now he spouted a brown stream into his special private spittoon. "Hard work? I *know*. I've damn near fucked cobras. That's how I got the pesetas to open this bar. But

I was doing it for myself. To make something of *me*. Aces, he's lost in the life. Right now he's here with Bab's bunch."

Tangier is a white piece of cubist sculpture displayed against a mountainside facing the Bay of Gibraltar. One descends from the top of the mountain, through a middle-class suburb sprinkled with ugly Mediterranean villas, to the "modern" town, a broiling miasma of overly wide boulevards, cement-colored high-rises, to the sleaky maze of the sea-coasted Casbah. Except for those present for presumably legitimate business purposes, virtually every foreign Tangerine is ensconced there for at least one, if not all, of four reasons: the easy availability of drugs, lustful adolescent prostitutes, tax loopholes, or because he is so undesirable, no place north of Port Said would let him out of the airport or off a ship. It is a dull town where all the essential risks have been removed.

At that time, the five reigning queens of the Casbah were two Englishmen and three American women. Eugenia Bankhead was among the females—a woman as original as her sister Tallulah, someone who made a mad sunshine of her own in the twilights of the harbor. And Jane Bowles, that genius imp, that laughing, hilarious, tortured elf. Author of a sinisterly marvelous novel, *Two Serious Ladies,* and of a single play, *In the Summer House,* of which the same description could be given, the late Mrs. Bowles lived in an infinitesimal Casbah house, a dwelling so small-scaled and low-ceilinged that one had almost to crawl from room to room; she lived there with her Moorish lover, the famous Cherifa, a rough old peasant woman who was the empress of herbs and rare spices at the largest of Tangier's open-air bazaars—an abrasive personality only a genius as witty and dedicated to extreme oddity as Mrs. Bowles could have abided. ("But," said Jane with a cherubic laugh, "I do love Cherifa. Cherifa doesn't love me. How could she? A writer? A crippled Jewish girl from Ohio? All she thinks about is money. My money. What little there is. And the house. And how to get the house. She tries very seriously to poison me at least every six months. And don't imagine I'm being paranoid. It's quite true.")

Mrs. Bowles' dollhouse was the reverse of the walled palace that belonged to the neighborhood's third genetically authentic queen, dime-store maharani Barbara Hutton—the Ma Barker of Bab's bunch, to quote Jay Hazlewood. Miss Hutton, with an entourage of temporary husbands, momentary lovers and others of unspecified (if any) occupation, usually reigned in her Moroccan mansion a month or so each year. Fragile, terrified, she rarely voyaged beyond its walls; exceedingly few locals were invited inside them. A wandering waif—Madrid today, Mexico tomorrow—Miss Hutton never traveled; she merely crossed frontiers, carting forty trunks and her insular *ambiente* with her.

"Hey there! How'd you like to go to a party?" Aces Nelson; he was calling to me from a café terrace in the Petit Socco, a Casbah piazza and great hubble-bubbling alfresco salon from noon to noon; it was past midnight now.

"Look," said Aces, who wasn't high on anything but his own

high spirits; in fact, he was drinking *the Arabé.* "I have a present for you." And he juggled in his hands a wiggling plump-stomached bitch puppy, an Afro-haired pickaninny with white rings circling both her big scared eyes—like a panda, some sort of ghetto panda. Aces said: "I bought her five minutes ago from a Spanish sailor. He was just walking past with this funny thing stuffed in the pocket of his pea jacket. Head flopping out. And I saw these lovely eyes. And these lovely ears—see, one drooping, the other perked up. I inquired, and he said his sister had sent him to sell it to Mr. Wu, the Chinaman who eats roasted dogs. So I offered a hundred pesetas; and here we are." Aces thrust the little dog at me, like a Calcutta beggar woman proffering an afflicted infant. "I didn't realize why I bought her until I saw you. Saunter-ing into the Socco. Mr. . . . Jones? Have I got that right? Here, Mr. Jones, take her. You need each other."

Dogs, cats, kids, I had never had anything dependent upon me; it was too time-consuming a chore just changing my own diapers. So I said: "Forget it. Give her to the Chinaman."

Aces leveled at me a gambler's gaze. He set the puppy on the center of the café table, where she stood a moment, trembling traumatically, then squatted to pee. Aces! You son of a bitch. *The nuns. The bluffs above St. Louis.* I picked her up and wrapped her in a Lanvin scarf Denny Fouts had given me long ago and held her close. She stopped trembling. She sniffed, sighed, slumbered.

Aces said: "And what are you going to name her?"

"Mutt."

"Oh? Since I brought you together, the least you might do is call her Aces."

"Mutt. Like her. Like you. Like me. Mutt."

He laughed. "*Alors*. But I promised you a party, Jones. Mrs. Cary Grant is minding the store tonight. It'll be a bore. But still."

Aces, at least behind her back, always referred to the Huttontot (a Winchell coinage) as Mrs. Cary Grant: "Out of respect, really. He was the only one of her husbands worthy of the name. He adored her; but she had to leave him: she can't trust or understand any geezer if he isn't after le loot."

A seven-foot Senegalese in a crimson turban and a white jellaba opened iron gates; one entered a garden where Judas trees blossomed in lantern light and the mesmeric scent of tuberoses embroidered the air. We passed into a room palely alive with light filtered through ivory filigree screens. Brocaded banquettes, piled with brocaded pillows of a silken lemon and silver and scarlet luxury, lined the walls. And there were beautiful brass tables shiny with candles and sweating champagne buckets; the floors, thick with overlapping layers of rugs from the weavers of Fez and Marrakech, were like strange lakes of ancient, intricate color.

The guests were few and all subdued, as though waiting for the hostess to retire before tossing themselves into an exuberant freedom—the repression attendant upon courtiers waiting for the royals to recede.

The hostess, wearing a green sari and a chain of dark emeralds, reclined among the cushions. Her eyes had the vacancy often observed in persons long imprisoned and, like her emeralds, a mineralized remoteness. Her eyesight, what she chose to see, was eerily selective: she saw me, but she never noticed the dog I was carrying.

"Oh, Aces dear," she said in a wan small voice. "What *have* you found now?"

"This is Mr. Jones. P. B. Jones, I believe."

"And you are a poet, Mr. Jones. Because I am a poet. And I can always tell."

And yet, in a touching, shrunken way, she was rather pretty— a prettiness marred by her seeming to be precariously balanced on the edge of pain. I remembered reading in some Sunday supplement that as a young woman she had been plump, a wallflower butterball, and that, at the suggestion of a diet faddist, she had swallowed a tapeworm or two; and now one wondered, because of the starved starkness, her feathery flimsiness, if those worms were not still gross tenants who accounted for half her present weight. Obviously she had somewhat read my mind: "Isn't it silly. I'm so thin, I'm too weak to walk. I have to be carried everywhere. Truly, I'd like to read your poetry."

"I'm not a poet. I'm a masseur."

She winced. "*Bruises.* A leaf drops and I'm blue."

Aces said: "You told me you were a writer."

"Well, I am. Was. Sort of. But it seems I'm a better masseur than a writer."

Miss Hutton consulted Aces; it was as if they were whispering with their eyes.

She said: "Perhaps he could help Kate."

He said, addressing me: "Are you free to travel?"

"Possibly. I don't seem to do much else."

"When could you meet me in Paris?" he asked, brisk now, a businessman.

"Tomorrow."

"No. Next week. Thursday. Ritz bar. Rue Cambon side. One-fifteen."

The heiress sighed into the banquette's goose-stuffed brocades. "Poor boy," she said, and tapped curving, slavishly lacquered apricot nails against a champagne glass, a signal for the Senegalese servant to lift her, lift her away up blue-tiled stairs to firelit chambers where Morpheus, always a mischief-maker to the frantic, the insulted, but especially to the rich and powerful, joyfully awaited a game of hide-and-seek.

I sold a sapphire ring, also a gift from Denny Fouts, who in turn had received it as a birthday present from his Grecian prince, to Dean, the mulatto proprietor of Dean's Bar, the principal rival of Le Parade for the colony's *haute monde* trade. It was a giveaway, but it flew me to Paris, and Mutt, too—Mutt stuffed into an Air France travel bag.

On Thursday, at one-fifteen precisely, I walked into the Ritz bar still toting Mutt in her canvas satchel, for she had refused to remain behind in the cheap hotel room we had moved into on the rue du Bac. Aces Nelson, slick-haired and gleamingly good-humored, was waiting for us at a corner table.

He patted the dog and said: "Well. I'm surprised. I didn't really think you'd show up."

All I said was: "This had better be good."

Georges, the head bartender at the Ritz, is a daiquiri specialist. I ordered a double daiquiri, so did Aces, and while they were being concocted, Aces asked: "What do you know about Kate McCloud?"

I shrugged. "Just what I read in the junk papers. Very handy with a rifle. Isn't she the one who shot a white leopard?"

"No," he said thoughtfully. "She was on safari in India, and she shot a man for killing a white leopard—not fatally, fortunately."

The drinks appeared, and we drank them without another word between us, except Mutt's intermittent yaps. A good daiquiri is smoothly tart and slightly sweet; a bad one is a vial of acid. Georges knew the difference. So we ordered another, and Aces said: "Kate has an apartment here in the hotel, and after we've talked I want you to meet her. She's expecting us. But first I want to tell you about her. Would you like a sandwich?"

We ordered plain chicken sandwiches, the only variety available in the Ritz bar, Cambon side. Aces said: "I had a roommate at Choate—Harry McCloud. His mother was an Otis from Baltimore, and his father owned a lot of Virginia—specifically, he owned a big spread in Middleburg, where he bred hunting horses.

Harry was very intense, a very competitive and jealous guy. But anybody as rich as he was, and as good-looking, athletic—you don't hear many complaints. Everybody took him for a regular guy, except for this one strange thing—whenever the guys started bullshitting about sex, girls they'd laid, wanted to lay, all that stuff, well, Harry kept his mouth shut. The whole two years we roomed together he never had a date, never mentioned a girl. Some of the guys said maybe Harry's queer. But I just knew that wasn't the case. It was a real mystery. Finally, the week before graduation, we got loaded on a bunch of beer—ah, sweet seventeen—and I asked if all his family were coming for the graduation, and he said: 'My brother is. And Mom and Dad.' Then I said: 'What about your girl friend? But I forgot. You don't have a girl friend.' He looked at me for the longest while, as if he were trying to decide whether to hit me or ignore me. At last he smiled; it was the fiercest smile I ever saw on a human face. I can't explain, but it stunned me; it made me want to cry. 'Yes. I have a girl friend. Nobody knows it. Not her folks, not mine. But we've been engaged for three years. The day I'm twenty-one I'm going to marry her. I'll be eighteen in July, and I'd marry her then. But I can't. She's only twelve years old.'

"Most secrets should never be told, but especially those that are more menacing to the listener than to the teller; I felt Harry would turn against me for having coaxed, or shall I say permitted, his confession. But once started, there was no surcease. He was incoherent, the incoherency of the obsessed: the girl's father, a

Mr. Mooney, was an Irish immigrant, a real bog rat from County Kildare, the hand groom at the McClouds' Middleburg farm. The girl, that's Kate, was one of five children, all girls, and all eyesores. Except for the youngest, Kate. 'The first time I saw her—well, *noticed* her—she was six, seven. All the Mooney kids had red hair. But *her* hair. Even all scissored up. Like a tomboy. She was a great rider. She could urge a horse into jumps that made your heart thump. And she had green eyes. Not *just* green. I can't explain it.'

"The senior McClouds had two sons, Harry and a younger boy, Wynn. But they had always wanted a daughter, and gradually, without any resistance from the girl's family, they had absorbed Kate into the main household. Mrs. McCloud was an educated woman, a linguist, musician, a collector. She tutored Kate in French and German and taught her piano. More importantly, she took all the ain'ts and Irish out of Kate's vocabulary. Mrs. McCloud dressed her, and on European holidays Kate traveled with the family. 'I've never loved anyone else.' That's what Harry said. 'Three years ago I asked her to marry me, and she promised she would never marry anyone else. I gave her a diamond ring. I stole it from my grandmother's jewel case. My grandmother decided she had lost it. She even claimed the insurance. Kate keeps the ring hidden in a trunk.' "

When the sandwiches arrived, Aces pushed his aside in favor of a cigarette. I ate half of mine and fed the rest to Mutt.

"And sure enough, four years later, Harry McCloud married

this extraordinary girl, scarcely sixteen. I went to the wedding—
it was at the Episcopal church in Middleburg—and the first time
I saw the bride was when she came down the aisle on the arm of
her little bog-rat dad. The truth is *she was some kind of freak.* The
grace, the bearing, the *authority:* whatever her age, she was simply
a superb actress. Are you a Raymond Chandler fan, Jones? Oh,
good. Good. I think he's a great artist. The point is, Kate Mooney
reminded me of one of those mysterious enigmatic rich-girl Raymond Chandler heroines. Oh, but with a lot more class. Anyway,
Chandler wrote about one of his heroines: 'There are blondes, and
then there are blondes.' So true; but it's even truer about redheads.
There is always something wrong with redheads. The hair is
kinky, or it's the wrong color, too dark and tough, or too pale and
sickly. And the skin—it rejects the elements: wind, sun, everything discolors it. A really beautiful redhead is rarer than a flawless
forty-carat pigeon-blood ruby—or a flawed one, for that matter.
But none of this was true of Kate. Her hair was like a winter
sunset, lighted with the last of the pale afterglow. And the only
redhead I've ever seen with a complexion to compare with hers
was Pamela Churchill's. But then, Pam is English, she grew up
saturated with dewy English mists, something every dermatolo-
gist ought to bottle. And Harry McCloud was quite right about
her eyes. Mostly it's a myth. Usually they are grey, grey-blue with
green inner flickerings. Once, in Brazil, I met on the beach a
light-skinned colored boy with eyes as slightly slanted and green
as Kate's. Like Mrs. Grant's emeralds.

85

"She was perfect. Harry worshiped her; so did his parents. But they had overlooked one small factor—she was shrewd, she could outthink any of them, and she was planning far beyond the McClouds. I recognized that at once. I belong to the same breed, though I can't pretend to have one-tenth Kate's intelligence."

Aces fished in his jacket pocket for a kitchen match; snapping it against his thumbnail, he ignited another cigarette.

"No," Aces said, responding to an unasked question. "They never had any children. Years passed, and I had cards from them every Christmas, usually a picture of Kate smartly saddled for some hunt—Harry holding the reins, bugle in hand. Bubber Hayden, a guy we'd known at Choate, turned up at one of those chatty little Joe Alsop Georgetown dinners; I knew he lived in Middleburg, so I asked him about the McClouds. Bubber said: 'She divorced him—she's gone abroad to live, I believe some three months ago. It's a terrible story, and I don't know a quarter of it. I do know the McClouds have Harry tucked away in one of those comfy little Connecticut retreats with guarded gates and strong bars at the windows.'

"I must have had that conversation in early August. I called Harry's mother—she was at the yearling sales in Saratoga—and I asked about Harry; I said I wanted to visit him, and she said no, that wasn't possible, and she began to cry and said she was sorry and hung up.

"Now, it happens that I was going to St. Moritz for Christmas; on the way I stopped off in Paris and called up Tutti Rouxjean, who had worked for years as *vendeuse* for Balenciaga. I invited her to lunch, and she said yes, but we would have to go to Maxim's. I said couldn't we meet at some quiet bistro, and she said no, we had to go to Maxim's. 'It's important. You'll see why.'

"Tutti had reserved a table in the front room, and after we'd had a glass of white wine she indicated a nearby unoccupied table rather ostentatiously set for one. 'Wait,' said Tutti. 'In a moment the most beautiful young woman will be sitting at that table, quite alone. Cristobal has been dressing her for the last six months. He thinks there has never been anything like her since Gloria Rubio.' (Note: Mme. Rubio, a supremely elegant Mexican who has been known in various stages of her marital assignments as the wife of the German Count von Fürstenberg, the Egyptian Prince Fakri, and the English millionaire Loel Guinness.) '*Le tout Paris* talks about her and yet no one knows much about her. Except that she's American. And that she lunches here every day. Always alone. She seems to have no friends. Ah, see. There she is.'

"Unlike any other woman in the room, she wore a hat. It was a glamorous soft-brimmed black hat, large, shaped like a man's Borsalino. A grey chiffon scarf was loosely knotted at her throat. The hat, the scarf, that was the drama; the rest was the plainest, but best-fitted, of Balenciaga's box-jacketed black bombazine suits.

"Tutti said: 'She's from the South somewhere. Her name is Mrs. McCloud.'

" 'Mrs. Harry Clinton McCloud?'

"Tutti said: 'You *know* her?'

"And I said: 'I ought to. I was an usher at her wedding. Fantastic. Why, my God, she can't be more than twenty-two.'

"I asked a waiter for paper and wrote her a note: 'Dear Kate, I don't know if you remember me, but I was a roommate of Harry's at school and an usher at your wedding. I am in Paris for a few days and would like so much to see you, if you care to. I am at the Hotel Lotti. Aces Nelson.'

"I watched her read the note, glance at me, smile, then write a reply: 'I do remember. If, on your way out, we might talk a minute alone, please have a Cognac with me. Most sincerely, Kate McCloud.'

"Tutti was too fascinated to be offended by her exclusion from the invitation: 'I won't press you now, but promise me, Aces, you'll tell me about her. She's the most beautiful woman I've ever seen. I thought she was at least thirty. Because of her "eye"—the real knowledge, taste. She's just one of those ageless creatures, I suppose.'

"And so, after Tutti had departed, I joined Kate at her solitary table, seated myself beside her on the red banquette, and to my surprise she kissed me on the cheek. I blushed with shock and pleasure, and Kate laughed—oh, what a laugh she has; it always makes me think of a brandy glass shining in the firelight—she laughed and said: 'Why not? It's been a long time since I've kissed a man. Or spoken to anyone who wasn't a waiter or chambermaid or a shopkeeper. I do a great deal of shopping. I've bought enough stuff to furnish Versailles.' I asked how long she had been in Paris and where she was living and what her life was like in general. And she said she was at the Ritz, she'd been in Paris almost a year: 'And as for my day-to-day affairs—I shop, I go for fittings, I go to all the museums and galleries, I ride to the Bois, I read, I sleep a helluva lot, and I have lunch here every day at this same table: not very imaginative of me, but it is a pleasant walk from the hotel, and there are not too many agreeable restaurants where a young woman can lunch alone without seeming somewhat suspicious. Even the owner here, Monsieur Vaudable—I think at first he imagined I must be some kind of courtesan.' And I said: 'But it must be such a lonely life. Don't you want to see people? Do something different?'

"She said: 'Yes. I'd like to have a different kind of liqueur with my coffee. Something I've never heard of. Any suggestions?'

"So I described Verveine; I thought of it because it is the identical green of her eyes. It's made out of a million-odd mountain herbs; I've never found it anywhere outside France and damn few places here. Delicious; but with a kick like bad moonshine. So we had a couple of Verveines, and Kate said: 'Yes, indeed. That certainly is different. And yes, to answer you seriously, I am beginning to be . . . well, not *bored*, but *tempted:* afraid, but tempted. When you've been in pain for a long time, when you wake up every morning with a rising sense of hysteria, then boredom is what you want, marathon sleeps, a silence in yourself. Everybody wanted me to go to a hospital; and I would have done anything to please Harry's mother, but I knew I could never live again, be *tempted*, until I'd tried to do it unaided by anyone but myself.'

"Suddenly I said: 'Are you a good skier?' And she said: 'I might have been. But Harry was always dragging me to this horrible place in Canada. Gray Rocks. Thirty below zero. He loved it because everybody was so ugly. Aces, this drink is a marvelous discovery. I feel a decided thawing in my veins.'

"Then I said: 'How would you like to spend Christmas with me in St. Moritz?' And she wanted to know: 'Is that a platonic invitation?' I crossed my heart. 'We'll stay at the Palace. On floors as far apart as you like.' She laughed and said: 'The answer is yes. But only if you'll buy me another Verveine.'

"That was six years ago—Lord, all the blood that's flowed under the bridge since then. But that first Christmas in St. Moritz! Really, the young Mrs. McCloud from Middleburg, Virginia, was one of the most important things that had happened in Switzerland since Hannibal crossed the Alps.

"In any event, she was a fabulous skier—as good as Doris Brynner or Eugénie Niarchos or Marella Agnelli: Kate and Eugénie and Marella became Bobbsey triplets. They used to helicopter up to the Corviglia Club every morning and have lunch and ski down in the afternoon. People loved her. The Greeks. The Persians. The Krauts. The Spaghettis. At every dinner party, the Shah invariably asked to have her at his table. And it wasn't just men—women, even the great rival young beauties like Fiona Thyssen and Dolores Guinness, reacted warmly, I think because

Bate's attitude was so carefully correct: she never flirted, and when she went to parties she went with me and left with me. A few idiots thought it was a romance, but the cleverer ones said, and rightly so, that a swan of Kate's feather would never bother with a backgammon bum like Aces Nelson.

"And anyway, I didn't aspire to be her lover. But a friend; a brother, perhaps. We used to go for snowy walks in the white forests around St. Moritz. She often talked about the McClouds and how good they'd been to her and to her sisters, the homely Mooney girls. But she avoided Harry's name, and when she did speak of him the references were casual, though bitter-tinted—until one afternoon, as we were strolling around the frozen lake beneath the palace, a passing sled horse slipped on the ice and fell and broke its front legs.

"Kate screamed. A scream you could have heard the length of the valley. She started to run, and ran straight into another sled that was rounding the corner. She wasn't physically wounded, but she went into a hysterical coma—she was virtually unconscious until we got her to the hotel. Mr. Badrutt had a doctor waiting. The doctor gave her an injection that seemed to start her heart again, refocus her eyes. He wanted to order a nurse, but I said no, I would stay with her. So we put her to bed, and he gave her another *piqûre*, one that totally erased all trace of terror; and it was then I realized that swimming below the soigné surface, there had always been a fearful, drowning child.

"I lowered the lights, and she said please don't leave me, and

I said I'm not leaving, I'm going to sit here, and she said no, I want you to lie down here beside me on the bed, so I did, and we held hands and she said: 'I'm sorry. It was because of the horse. The one that fell on the ice. I'd always wanted a palomino, and Mrs. McCloud gave me one on my birthday two years ago, a mare—such a great hunter, so brave-hearted; we had such fun together. Naturally, Harry hated her; it was all part of his crazy-man jealousy, the way he'd felt toward me since we were children. Once, the summer after we were married, he tore up a flower garden I'd planted; at first he said it was a fox, but then he admitted he had done it: he said the garden took up too much of my attention. And that was why he didn't want me to have a baby; his mother was always bringing up the subject, and one Sunday at dinner, right in front of the whole family, he shouted at her: "Do you want a *black* grandchild? Or don't you people know about Kate? She fucks niggers. She goes out in the fields and lies down and fucks niggers." He went to law school at Washington and Lee and flunked out because he couldn't concentrate unless he had me under surveillance; he opened and read all my letters even before I had a chance to see them; he monitored all my telephone calls: you could always hear him slightly breathing at the other end of the line. We'd long since stopped being invited to parties; we couldn't even go to the country club—drunk or sober, Harry was ready to throw a punch, usually at some man who had asked me to dance more than once. The worst of it—he was convinced that I was having an affair with his father and with his brother, Wynn.

A hundred nights he shook me and woke me up, holding a knife at my throat—and he'd say: "Don't lie to me, you slut, you whore, you nigger-fucker. Admit it, or I'll cut your throat from ear to ear. I'll slice your head off. Tell the truth. Wynn's a real stud, the best you've ever had, and Dad, too, he's a great stallion." We'd lie like that for hours, Aces—that cold knife at my throat. Mrs. McCloud, everybody, knew about it; but Mrs. McCloud would cry and beg me not to leave, she was so sure Harry would kill himself if I did. Then the thing happened about my palomino, Nanny. Even Mrs. McCloud had to open her eyes to the real extent of Harry's insanity—this insane jealousy. Because what Harry did was, he went down to the stable and he broke all of Nanny's legs with a crowbar. Even Mrs. McCloud saw it was useless, that Harry would kill me sooner or later; she chartered a plane and we flew out to Sun Valley, where she stayed with me the whole while it took to get an Idaho divorce. A wonderful woman; I called her Christmas Day, and she was happy I was in St. Moritz and going out and seeing people: she wanted to know if I'd met any interesting men. As if I'd ever marry again!'

"But you know," said Aces, "she did marry. And less than a month later."

Yes: I was remembering a mass of magazine covers at Paris kiosks: *Der Stern, Paris Match, Elle.* "Of course. She married . . . ?"

"Axel Jaeger. The richest man in Germany."

"And she has since divorced Herr Jaeger?"

"Not exactly. That's one of the reasons I wanted you to meet her. She's in considerable danger. She needs protection. She also needs a masseur who can travel with her permanently. Someone educated. Presentable."

"I'm not educated."

He shrugged and glanced at his watch. "May I ring her now and say we're on our way up?"

I should have listened to Mutt; she whined, as if warning me. Instead, I let myself be led off to meet Kate McCloud. Kate, for whom I would lie, steal, commit crimes that could have, and still could, put me in prison for life.

A weather change; showers—an enlivening spray dispelling Manhattan's heat-wave stench. Not that anything could ever get rid of the jockstrap and Lysol aromas here at my beloved Y.M.C.A. I slept till noon, then called The Self Service to cancel a six P.M. booking they had made for me with some john staying at the Yale Club. But the sun-kissed bitch, the golden Butch, said: "Are you gaga? This is a C-note gig. A Benjy Franklin with no problems." When I still demurred ("Honest, Butch, I've got a blue-balls headache"), he put Miss Self *herself* on the phone, and she gave me a real Buchenwald, Ilse Koch castigation ("Ah, so? You want to work? You don't want? Dilettantes we don't need!").

Okay, okay. I showered, shaved, and arrived at the Yale Club with a button-down collar, clipped hair, discreet, not fat, not femme, aged between thirty and forty, fairly well-hung and well-mannered: just what the john had ordered.

He seemed pleased with me; and it was no hassle—a reclining labor, shuttered eyes, occasionally a spurious appreciative grunt as one fantasized toward the obligatory spasm ("Don't hold back. Let me have it").

The "patron," to use Miss Self's terminology, was hearty, balding, hard as a walnut, a man in his middle sixties, married, with five children and eighteen grandchildren. A widower, he had married his secretary, someone twenty years younger, perhaps a decade ago. He was a retired insurance executive who owned a farm near Lancaster, Pennsylvania, where he bred cattle, and, as a hobby, "unusual" roses. He told me all this while I was dressing. I liked him, and what I liked most was that he didn't ask me a single question about myself. As I was leaving, he gave me his card (unique for the anonymity-aware Self Service clients) and said if I ever felt like dusting the city off my heels to ring him up: I was welcome to vacation at Appleton Farms. His name was Roger W. Appleton, and Mrs. Appleton, he informed me with a pleasant, entirely unvulgar wink, was an understanding woman: "Alice is a fine person. But restless. She reads a lot." By which I understood that he was suggesting a threesome. We shook hands—his handshake was so muscular my knuckles were numb a solid minute— and I promised I'd think about it. Hell, it was something to consider: meandering cattle, green meadows, roses, the absence of . . .

All this! Snores. Soiled breathings. Asphyxiation. The lugubrious slapslap of searching feet. On my way "home," ha ha, I bought a pint of clearance-sale gin—the kind of raw ambrosia that would gag a slew of skid-row throats. I killed half of it in two gulps, then began to nod, began to remember Denny Fouts and to wish I could dash downstairs and find a bus, the Magic Mushroom Express, a chartered torpedo that would rocket me to the end of the line, zoom me all the way to that halycon discotheque: Father Flanagan's Nigger Queen Kosher Café.

Stop. You're pissed, P. B. You're a loser, an asshole dumb drunk loser, P. B. Jones. So good night. Good night, Walter Winchell —in whatever hell you're baking. Good night, Mr. and Mrs. America and all the ships at sea—in whatever sea you're sinking. And a very special good night to that wise philosopher Florie Rotondo, age eight. Florie—and I mean this, honey—I hope you never reached the interior of the planet Earth, never discovered uranium, rubies, and Unspoiled Monsters. With all my heart, what there is of it, I hope you moved to the country and lived there happily ever after.

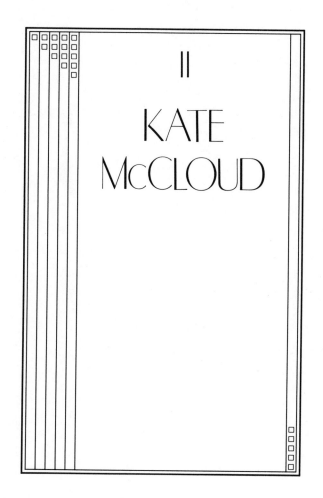

II

KATE
McCLOUD

"I may be a black sheep, but my hooves are made of gold"

P. B. JONES,
while under the influence

*D*uring the week my sainted employer, Miss Victoria Self, sent me out on seven "dates" within three days, even though I pleaded everything from bronchitis to gonorrhea. And now she's trying to talk me into appearing in a porno film ("P. B. Listen, darling. It's a class production. With a *script.* I can get you two hundred a day"). But I don't want to go into all that, not just now.

Anyway, last night I felt too ripple-blooded, too restless to sleep; it was impossible, I just couldn't lie awake here in my so-divine Y.M.C.A. cell listening to the midnight farts and night-mare moanings of my Christian brethren.

So I decided to walk over to West 42nd Street, which isn't far from here, and search out a movie at one of those ammonia-scented all-night movie palaces. It was after one when I set out, and the route of my walk carried me along nine blocks of Eighth

Avenue. Prostitutes, blacks, Puerto Ricans, a few whites, and indeed all strata of street-people society—the luxurious Latin pimps (one wearing a white mink hat and a diamond bracelet), the heroin-nodders nodding in doorways, the male hustlers, among the boldest of them gypsy boys and Puerto Ricans and runaway hillbilly rednecks no more than fourteen and fifteen years old ("Mister! Ten dollars! Take me home! Fuck me all night!")—circled the sidewalks like buzzards above an abattoir. Then the occasional cruising cop car, its passengers uninterested, unseeing, having seen it all until their eyes are rheumy with the sight.

I passed The Loading Zone, an S & M bar at 40th and Eighth, and there was a gang of laughing, howling, leather-jacketed, leath-er-helmeted jackals crowded on the sidewalk surrounding a young man, costumed exactly as they were, who, unconscious, was sprawled between the curb and the sidewalk, where all his friends, colleagues, tormentors, whatever the hell you care to call them, were urinating on him, drenching him from head to heel. Nobody noticed; well, *noticed*, but merely enough to slow their movement slightly; they kept walking—all except a bunch of indignant prostitutes, black, white, and at least half of them transvestites, who kept shouting at the urinators ("Stop that! Oh, stop that! You *fairies*. You dirty fairies!") and slapping them with their purses—until the leather-boys started hosing them down, laughing the louder, and the "girls," in their stretch pants and surrealist wigs (blueberry, strawberry, vanilla, Afro-gold) ran in flutterbutt flight down the street shrieking, but enjoyably so: "Fags. Fairies. Dirty mean fags."

They hesitated at the street corner to heckle a preacher, or an orator of sorts, who, like an exorcist demolishing demons, was assaulting a shifting, shiftless audience of sailors and hustlers, drug-pushers and beggars, and white-trash farm boys freshly arrived at the Port Authority bus terminal. "Yes! Yes!" screamed the preacher, the flickering lights of a hot-dog stand greening his young, taut, hungry, hysterical face. "The devil is wallowing inside you," he screamed, his Oklahoma voice thorny as barbed wire. "The devil squats there, fat, feeding on your evil. Let the light of the Lord starve him out. Let the light of the Lord lift you to heaven—"

"Oh yeah?" yelled one of the whores. "Ain't no Lord gonna lift nobody heavy as *you*. You too full of shit."

The preacher's mouth twisted with lunatic resentment. "Scumbags! Filth."

A voice answered him: "Shut up. Don't call them names."

"What?" said the preacher, screaming again.

"I'm no better than they are. And you are no better than I am. We're all the same person." And suddenly I realized the voice was *mine,* and I thought boyoboy, Jesus, kid, you're losing your marbles, your brains are running out of your ears.

So I hurried right into the first theatre I came to, not bothering to notice what films were on display. In the lobby I bought a chocolate bar and a bag of buttered popcorn—I hadn't eaten since breakfast. Then I found a seat in the balcony, which was an error, for it is in the balconies of these round-the-clock emporiums that the shadows of tireless sex-searchers weave and wander among the rows—wrecked whores, women in their sixties and seventies who want to blow you for a dollar ("Fifty cents?"), and men who offer the same service for nothing, and other men, sometimes rather conservative executive types, who seem to specialize in accosting the numerous slumbering drunks.

Then, there on the screen I saw Montgomery Clift and Elizabeth Taylor. *An American Tragedy,* a film I'd seen at least twice, not that it was all that great, but still it was very good, especially the final scene, which was unreeling at this particular moment: Clift and Taylor standing together, separated by the bars of a prison cell, a death cell, for Clift is only hours away from execution. Clift, already a poetic ghost inside his grey death-clothes, and Taylor, nineteen and ravishing, sublimely fresh as lilac after rain. Sad. *Sad.* Enough to jerk the tears out of Caligula's eyes. I choked on a mouthful of popcorn.

The picture ended, and was immediately replaced by *Red River,* a cowboy love story starring John Wayne and, once again, Montgomery Clift. It was Clift's first important film role, the one that made him a "star"—as I had good reason to recall.

Remember Turner Boatwright, the late, not too lamented magazine editor, my old mentor (and nemesis), the dear fellow who got beaten by a dope-crazed Latino until his heart stopped and his eyes popped out of his head?

One morning, while I was still in his good graces, he telephoned and invited me to dinner: "Just a little party. Six altogether. I'm giving it for Monty Clift. Have you seen his new picture—*Red River?*" he asked, and went on to explain that he'd known Clift a long time, ever since he was a very young actor, a protégé of the Lunts. "So," said Boaty, "I asked him if there was any particular person he wanted me to invite and he said yes, Dorothy Parker—he'd always wanted to meet Dorothy Parker. And I thought oh my God—because Dottie's become such a lush, you never know when her face is going to land in the soup. But I rang up Dottie and she said oh she'd be *thrilled* to come. She thought Monty was the most beautiful young man she'd ever seen. 'But I can't,' she said, 'because I've already promised to have dinner with Tallulah that evening. And you know how she is: she'd ride me on a rail if I begged off.' So I said listen, Dottie, let me handle this: I'll call Tallulah and invite her, too. And that's what happened. Tallulah said she'd love to come, d-d-darling, except for one thing—she'd already invited Estelle Winwood, and could she bring Estelle?"

It was a heady notion, the thought of these three formidable ladies all in one room: Bankhead, Dorothy Parker, and Estelle Winwood. Boaty's invitation was for seven-thirty, allowing an hour for cocktails before dinner, which he had prepared himself —Senegalese soup, a casserole, salad, assorted cheeses, and a lemon soufflé. I arrived somewhat early to see if I could be of any help, but Boaty, wearing an olive velvet jacket, was calm, everything was in order, there was nothing left to do except light the candles.

The host poured each of us one of his "special" martinis—gin of zero temperature to which a drop of Pernod had been added. "No vermouth. Just a touch of Pernod. An old trick I learned from Virgil Thompson."

Seven-thirty became eight; by the time we had our second drink the other guests were more than an hour late, and Boaty's sleekly knitted composure began to unravel; he started nibbling at his fingernails, a most uncharacteristic indulgence. At nine he exploded: "My God, do you realize what I've *done?* I don't know about Estelle, but the other three are all drunks. I've invited three alcoholics to dinner! *One* is bad enough. But *three.* They'll never show up."

The doorbell rang.

"D-d-darling . . ." It was Miss Bankhead, gyrating inside a mink coat the color of her long, loosely waved hair. "I'm so sorry. It was all the taxi-driver's fault. He took us to the wrong address. Some wretched apartment house on the *West* Side."

Miss Parker said: "Benjamin Katz. That was his name. The taxi-driver."

"You're wrong, Dottie," Miss Winwood corrected her as the ladies discarded their coats and were escorted by Boaty into his dark Victorian parlor, where logs were cheerfully crunching inside a marble fireplace. "His name was Kevin O'Leary. Badly suffering from the Irish virus. That's why he didn't know where he was going."

"Irish virus?" said Miss Bankhead.

"Booze, dear," said Miss Winwood.

"Ah, booze," sighed Miss Parker. "That's exactly what I need," though a slight sway in her walk suggested that another drink was exactly what she didn't need. Miss Bankhead ordered: "A bourbon and branch. And don't be stingy." Miss Parker, complaining of a certain *crise de foie,* at first declined, then said: "Well, perhaps a glass of wine."

Miss Bankhead, spying me where I stood by the fireplace, swooped forward; she was a small woman, but, because of her growling voice and unconquerable vitality, seemed Amazonian. "*And,* " she said, blink-blinking her near-sighted eyes, "is this Mr. Clift, our great new star?"

I told her no, that my name was P. B. Jones. "I'm nobody. Just a friend of Mr. Boatwright's."

"Not one of his 'nephews'?"

"No. I'm a writer, or want to be."

"Boaty has so many nephews. I wonder where he finds them all. Damn it, Boaty, where's my bourbon?"

As the guests settled among Boaty's horsehair settees, I decided that of the three, Estelle Winwood, an actress then in her early sixties, was the most striking. Parker—she looked like the sort of woman to whom one would instantly relinquish a subway seat, a vulnerable, deceptively incapable child who had gone to sleep and awakened forty years later with puffy eyes, false teeth, and whiskey on her breath. And Bankhead—her head was too large for her body, her feet too small; and anyway, her presence was too strong for a room to contain: it needed an auditorium. But Miss Winwood was an exotic creature—snake-slim, erect as a headmistress, she wore a huge broad-brimmed black straw hat which she never removed the entire evening; that hat's brim shadowed the pearl-pallor of her haughty face, and concealed, though not too successfully, the mischief faintly firing her lavender eyes. She was smoking a cigarette, and it developed that she was a chain-smoker, as was Miss Bankhead; Miss Parker, too.

Miss Bankhead lit one cigarette from another, and announced: "I had a strange dream last night. I dreamt I was at the Savoy in London. Dancing with Jock Whitney. Now *there* was an attractive man. Those big red ears, those dimples."

Miss Parker said: "Well? And what was so strange about that?"

"Nothing. Except that I haven't thought about Jock in twenty years. And then this very afternoon I *saw* him. He was crossing 57th Street in one direction, and I was going in the other. He hadn't changed much—a little heavier, a bit jowly. God, the great times we had together. He used to take me to the ball games; and the races. But it was never any good in bed. The same old story. I once went to an analyst and wasted fifty dollars an hour trying to figure out why I can never make it work with any man I really

love, am really mad about. While some stagehand, somebody I
don't give a damn about, can leave me limp."

Boaty appeared with the drinks; Miss Parker emptied her glass
with one swift swallow, then said: "Why don't you just bring the
bottle and leave it on the table?"

Boaty said: "I can't understand what's happened to Monty. At
least he could have called."

"Meeow! Meeow." The cat-wail was accompanied by the
sound of fingernails scratching against the front door. "Meeow!"

"*Pardonnez-moi, señor,*" said young Mr. Clift, as he fell into the
room and supported himself by hugging Boaty. "I've been sleeping off a hangover." Offhand, I would have said he hadn't slept
it off sufficiently. When Boaty offered him a martini, I noticed
that his hands trembled as he struggled to hold it.

Underneath a rumpled raincoat, he wore grey flannel slacks
and a grey turtle-neck sweater; he was also wearing argyle socks
and a pair of loafers. He kicked off the shoes and squatted at Miss
Parker's feet.

"The story of yours I like, I like the one about the woman who
keeps waiting for the telephone to ring. Waiting for a guy who's
trying to give her the brush. And she keeps making up reasons
why he doesn't call, and pleading with herself not to call him. I
know all about that. I've lived through it. And that other story—
"Big Blonde"—where the woman swallows all those pills, only
she doesn't die, she wakes up and has to go on living. Wow, I'd

hate to have that happen. Did you ever know anyone that happened to?"

Miss Bankhead laughed. "Of course she does. Dottie's always gulping pills or cutting her wrists. I remember going to see her in the hospital once, she had her wrists bandaged with pink ribbon with cute little pink ribbon bows. Bob Benchley said: 'If she doesn't stop doing that, Dottie's going to hurt herself one of these days.' "

Miss Parker complained: "Benchley didn't say that. *I* did. I said: 'If I don't stop doing this, someday I'm going to hurt myself.' "

For the next hour Boaty waddled between the kitchen and the parlor, fetching drinks and more drinks, and grieving over his dinner, particularly the casserole, which was drying out. It was after ten before he persuaded the others to arrange themselves around the dining-room table, and I helped by pouring the wine, the only nourishment that seemed to interest anyone, anyway: Clift dropped a cigarette into his untouched bowl of Senegalese soup, and stared inertly into space, as if he were enacting a shell-shocked soldier. His companions pretended not to notice, and Miss Bankhead continued a meandering anecdote ("It was when I had a house in the country, and Estelle was staying with me, and we were stretched out on the lawn listening to the radio. It was a portable radio, one of the first ever made. Suddenly a newscaster broke in; he said to stand by for an important announcement. It turned out to be about the Lindbergh kidnapping. How someone had used a ladder to climb into a bedroom and steal the baby.

When it was over, Estelle yawned and said: 'Well, we're well out of *that* one, Tallulah!' "). While she talked, Miss Parker did something so curious it attracted everyone's attention; it even silenced Miss Bankhead. With tears in her eyes, Miss Parker was touching Clift's hypnotized face, her stubby fingers tenderly brushing his brow, his cheekbones, his lips, chin.

Miss Bankhead said: "Damn it, Dottie. Who do you think you are? Helen Keller?"

"He's so beautiful," murmured Miss Parker. "Sensitive. So finely made. The most beautiful young man I've ever seen. What a pity he's a cocksucker." Then, sweetly, wide-eyed with little girl naïveté, she said: "Oh. Oh dear. Have I said something *wrong?* I mean, he is a cocksucker, isn't he, Tallulah?"

Miss Bankhead said: "Well, d-d-darling, I r-r-really wouldn't know. He's never sucked *my* cock."

I couldn't keep my eyes open; it was very boring, *Red River,* and the odor of latrine disinfectant was chloroforming me. I needed a drink, and I found one in an Irish bar at 38th Street and Eighth Avenue. It was almost closing time, but a jukebox was still going and a sailor was dancing to it all by himself. I ordered a triple gin. As I opened my wallet, a card fell out of it. A white business card containing a man's name, address, and telephone number: Roger W. Appleton Farms, Box 711, Lancaster, Pa. Tel: 905-537-1070. I stared at the card, wondering how it had come into my possession. Appleton? A long swallow of gin brightened my memory. Appleton. Of course. We had a Self Service client, one of the few I could recall pleasantly. We had spent an hour together in his room at the Yale Club; an older man, but weathered, strong, well-built, and with a handshake that was a real bone-cruncher. A nice guy, very open—he had told me a lot about himself: after his first wife died, he had married a much younger woman, and they lived on the lands of a rolling farm filled with fruit trees and roaming cows and narrow tumbling creeks. He had given me his card and told me to call him up and come for a visit any time. Embraced by self-pity, emboldened by alcohol, and totally forgetful of the fact that it must be three in the morning, I asked the bartender to give me five dollars' worth of quarters.

"Sorry, sonny. But we're shutting down."

"Please. This is an emergency. I've got to make a long-distance call."

Counting out the money, he said: "Whoever she is, she ain't worth it."

After I had dialed the number, an operator requested an additional four dollars. The phone rang half a dozen times before a woman's voice, deep and slow with sleep, responded.

"Hello. Is Mr. Appleton there?"

She hesitated. "Yes. But he's asleep. But if it's something important . . ."

"No. It's nothing important."

"May I ask who's calling?"

"Just tell him . . . just say a friend called. His friend from across the River Styx."

But to return to that winter afternoon in Paris when I first met Kate McCloud. There we were, the three of us—myself, my young mongrel dog, Mutt, and Aces Nelson, all clumped together inside one of those little silk-lined Ritz elevators.

We rode to the top floor, disembarked there, and as we walked along the corridor lined with old-fashioned steamer trunks, Aces said: "Of course, she doesn't know the real reason why I'm bringing you here . . ."

"If it comes to that, neither do I!"

"All I said was that I'd found this wonderful masseur. You see, for the last year she's been suffering from a back ailment. She's gone from doctor to doctor, here and in America. Some say it's a slipped disc, or a spinal fusion, but most agree it's psychosomatic, a *maladie imaginaire*. But the problem is . . ." His voice hovered.

"Is?"

"But I told you. Just now. While we were having drinks in the bar."

Segments of our conversation replayed inside my head. At present, Kate McCloud was the estranged wife of Axel Jaeger, a German industrialist and allegedly one of the world's richest men. Earlier, when she was sixteen, she had been married to the son of a rich Virginia horse breeder for whom her Irish father had worked as a trainer. That marriage had ended on very well-founded grounds of mental cruelty. Subsequently she had moved to Paris, and over the years, became a goddess of the fashion press; Kate McCloud on a bearhunt in Alaska, on a safari in Africa, at a Rothschild ball, at the Grand Prix with Princess Grace, on a yacht with Stavros Niarchos.

"The problem is . . ." Aces fumbled. "It's as I told you, she is in danger. And she needs . . . well, someone to be with her. A bodyguard."

"Hell, why don't we just sell her Mutt?"

"Please," he said. "This isn't humorous."

Those were the truest words old Aces had ever spoken. If only I could have foreseen the labyrinth he was leading me into when a black woman opened the door. She wore a smart black pants suit with numerous gold chains twisted around her neck and wrists. Her mouth was loaded with gold, too; her denture looked less like teeth than an investment. She had curly white hair and a round, unlined face. Asked to guess her age, I would have said forty-five, forty-six; later, I learned she was a child-bride.

"Corinne!" exclaimed Aces, and kissed the woman on both cheeks. *"Comment ça va?"*

"Never felt better, and never had less."

"P. B., this is Corinne Bennett, Mrs. McCloud's factotum. And, Corinne, this is Mr. Jones, the masseur."

Corinne nodded, but her eyes concentrated on the dog tucked under my arm. "What I want to know is, who is that dog? No present for Miss Kate, I hope. She's been muttering about getting another dog ever since Phoebe—"

"*Phoebe?*"

"Had to put her down. Same as they will me someday soon. But don't mention it to *her*. It'll just set her off again. Have mercy, I never saw a grown person cry that bad. Come along, she's waiting for you." Then, lowering her voice, she added: "That Mme. Apfeldorf is with her."

Aces grimaced; he looked at me as if about to speak, but there was no need; I'd leafed through enough *Vogue*'s and *Paris-Match*'s to know who Perla Apfeldorf was. The wife of a very racist South African platinum tycoon, she was as much a figure of the worldly milieu as Kate McCloud. She was Brazilian, and privately—though this was something I discovered later—her friends called her the Black Duchess, suggesting she was not of the pure Portuguese descent she claimed, but a child of Rio's *favelos*, born with quite a bit of the tarbrush which, if true, was rather a joke on the Hitlerian Herr Apfeldorf.

The apartment snuggled under the eaves of the hotel; the rooms, all dominated by large round dormer windows overlooking the Place Vendôme, were identical in size; originally they had been used as individual servant's rooms, but Kate McCloud had strung six of them together and decorated each for a particular purpose. The effect, overall, was like a railroad flat in a luxurious tenement.

"Miss Kate? The gentlemen are here."

And, magically, there we were inside Kate McCloud's bed-room. "Aces. Angel." She was perched on the side of a bed brushing her hair. "Will you have some tea? Perla's having some. Or a liqueur? No? Then I shall. Corinne, would you bring me a drop of Verveine? Aces, aren't you going to introduce me to Mr. Jones? Mr. Jones," she confided to Mme. Apfeldorf, who was seated in a chair beside the bed, "is going to drive the demons out of my spine."

"Well," said Mme. Apfeldorf, who had slicked-black hair shiny as a crow's and a voice with a crowlike croak, "I hope he's better than that sadistic little Japanese Mona sent my way. I'll never trust Mona again. Not that I ever did. You wouldn't believe what happened! He made me lie naked on the floor and then, in his bare feet, he *stood* on my neck, walked up and down my back, posi-tively danced. The *agony.*"

"Oh, Perla," said Kate McCloud pityingly. "What do you know about agony? I've just spent a week at St. Moritz and never saw a pair of skis. Never left my room except to visit Heinie. Just lay there munching Doridens and praying. Aces," she said, hand-ing him a silver frame that had been standing on a table near her bed, "here's a new picture of Heinie. Isn't he lovely?"

"This is Mrs. McCloud's son," Aces explained, showing me the picture in the frame: a chubby-cheeked solemn child muffled in mufflers and a fur coat and fur hat and holding a snowball. And then I noticed that placed around the room, there were really dozens of pictures of this same boy at varying ages.

"Lovely. How old is he now?"

"Five. Well, he'll be five in April." She resumed brushing her hair, but harshly, destructively. "It was a nightmare. I was never allowed once to see him alone. Dear Uncle Frederick and beloved Uncle Otto. The two old maids. They were always there. Watching. Counting the kisses and ready to show me the door the moment my hour was up." She threw the brush across the room, which made Mutt bark. "My own baby."

The Black Duchess cleared her throat; it sounded like a crow gargling. She said: "Kidnap him."

Kate McCloud laughed and collapsed against a heap of Porthault pillows. "Odd, though. You're the second person who's said that to me within the past week." She lit a cigarette. "It isn't quite true that I never went out in St. Moritz. I did. Twice. Once to dinner for the Shah, and another night some crazy fling Mingo had at the King's Club. And I met this extraordinary woman—"

Mme. Apfeldorf said: "Was Dolores there?"

"Where?"

"At the Shah's party."

"There were so many people, I can't remember. Why?"

"Nothing. Just rumors. Who gave it?"

Kate McCloud shrugged. "One of the Greeks. The Livanos, I think. And after dinner His Highness pulled his old stunt: kept everybody sitting at their table for hours while he told tasteless jokes. In French. English. German. Persian. Everybody howling with laughter, even if they hadn't understood a word. It's painful to watch Farah Diba; she really blushes—"

"Sounds as though he hasn't changed much since we were at school together in Gstaad. Le Rosey."

"And I had Niarchos sitting next to me, which was no help. He had enough Cognac in him to pickle a rhinoceros. He started at me, very belligerently, and said: 'Look me in the eye.' Well, I couldn't—his eyes were unfocused. 'Look me in the eye and tell me what makes you happiest in the world?' I told him sleep. He said: '*Sleep*. That's the saddest thing I've ever heard. You'll have thousands of years to sleep. Now I'll tell you what makes me happiest. To hunt. To kill. Prowl through the jungles and kill a tiger, an elephant, a lion. Then I am a peaceful man. Happy. What do you say to that?' And I said: "That's the saddest thing *I've* ever heard. To kill and destroy, that seems to me a very pathetic thing to call happiness.' "

The Black Duchess inclined her head, agreeing: "Yes, the Greeks are dark-minded. The rich Greeks. They bear the same resemblance to humans as coyotes do to dogs. Coyotes *look* like dogs; but of course they aren't dogs—"

Aces intervened to comment: "But, Kate, you like to hunt. How do you account for that?"

"I like to *play* at hunting. I like the walking and the wilderness. The only thing I ever shot was a Kodiak bear, and that was in self-defense."

"You shot a man," Aces reminded her.

"Only in the legs. And he deserved it. He killed a white leopard." Corinne appeared with a small glass of Verviene, and Aces
was right—the liqueur matched perfectly the ultra-green of her
eyes. "But what I started to tell you about was this amazing
woman I met at Mingo's fandango. She sat down next to me, and
said: 'Hello, honey. I hear you're a Southern girl, and so am I. I'm
from Alabama. I'm Virginia Hill.'"

Aces said: "*The* Virginia Hill?"

"Well, I didn't realize she was all that famous until Mingo told
me. I'd never heard of her."

"Nor I," said Mme. Apfeldorf. "Who is she? An actress?"

"A gangster's moll," Aces informed her. "The Most Wanted
woman. The F.B.I. have pictures of her posted in every post office
in America. I read an article about her, it was called 'The Ma-
donna of the Underworld.' Everybody's after her, not only the
F.B.I. but most of her old gangster chums, too: they figure if the
F.B.I. ever catch her, she might talk and talk too much. When
things got too tough, she fled to Mexico and married an Austrian
ski instructor; she's been holed up in Austria and Switzerland ever
since. The Americans have never been able to extradite her."

"*Mon Dieu,*" said Mme. Apfeldorf, making a sign of the cross.
"She must be a very frightened woman."

"Not frightened. Despairing, even suicidal perhaps; but she
wears a jovial mask very convincingly. She kept putting her arm
around me, squeezing me and saying: 'It sure is good to talk to
somebody from down home. Hell, you can take the whole of

Europe and cram it up your shithole. See my hand?' She showed me her hand; it was wrapped in plaster and gauze, and she said: 'I caught my husband in bed with one of these ladeda bimbos, and I broke her jaw. I would've broken his, too. If he hadn't jumped out the window. I guess you know all about my troubles stateside; but sometimes I feel I'd be better off to go home and get it over with. I can't be more in a jail there than I am here.' "

Aces said: "But what was she *really* like? Is she beautiful?"

Kate considered. "Never beautiful, but pretty, cute, like a cute little carhop. She has a nice face, but two chins to go with it. And I can't imagine what her tits weigh—at least a couple of kilos."

"Please, Kate," complained the Black Duchess. "You know how I dislike those words. Tits."

"Oh, yes. I always forget. You were educated by Brazilian nuns. Anyway, what I started to say was, suddenly this woman pressed her lips against my ear and whispered: 'Why don't you kidnap him?' I simply looked at her; I had no idea what she was talking about. She said: 'You know all about me but I know quite a lot about you. How you married that Kraut bastard and how he kicked you out and kept the kid. Listen, I'm a mother, too. I have a boy. And I know how you feel. With his money, and these European laws, the only way you're going to get that kid back is by kidnapping him.' "

Mutt whined; Aces jingled some coins in his pocket; Mme. Apfeldorf said: "I think she's quite correct. And it could be done."

"Yes, it could," said Aces. "A damned dangerous business. But it *could* be done."

"How?" Kate McCloud shouted, pounding her fists into the pillows. "You know that house. It's a fortress. I could never get him out of there. Not with old-maid uncles always watching. And the servants."

Aces said: "Still, that part of it might be accomplished. With exemplary planning."

"And then what? Once the alarm was sounded, I'd never get within ten miles of the Swiss frontier."

"But suppose," croaked Mme. Apfeldorf, "suppose you didn't try to cross the frontier. By car, I mean. Suppose you had a private Grumman jet waiting for you in the valley. All aboard, and off we go."

"To where?"

"To America!"

Aces was excited: "Yes! Yes! Once you were in the States, Herr Jaeger would be helpless. You could file for divorce, and there's no judge in America who wouldn't give you custody of Heinie."

"Daydreams. Pipedreams. Mr. Jones," she said, "I'm sorry to have kept you waiting so long. The massage table is in the closet over there."

"Pipedreams. Perhaps. But I'd think about it," said the Black Duchess, rising. "let's have lunch next week."

Aces kissed Kate McCloud on the cheek. "I'll call you later, darling. Take good care of my girl, P. B. And when you're finished, look me up in the bar."

While I was setting up the massage table, Mutt jumped on the bed and squatted to peepee. I started to grab her. "No harm. Many worse things have happened in this bed. She's so ugly she's adorable. I love her black face with those big white circles around her eyes. Like a Panda. How old is he?"

"Three, maybe four months. Mr. Nelson gave her to me."

"I wish he'd given her to *me*. What's her name?"

"Mutt."

"You can't call her *that*. She's far too charming. Let's think of something more suitable."

When I had the massage table arranged, she rolled off the bed and dropped a gauzy short negligee, underneath which she was nude. Her pubic hair and her shoulder-length honey-red hair were an exact color match; she was an authentic redhead, all right. She was thin, but her body needed not an extra ounce; because of the perfection of her posture, she seemed taller than she was —about my height: five feet eight inches. Casually, her perky breasts scarcely quivering, she crossed the room and touched the button of a stereo phonograph: Spanish music, Segovia's guitar, relieved the silence. Silently, she approached the massage table and reclined there, letting her fascinating hair fall over its end-edge. Sighing, she curtained her brilliant eyes; closed them as though she were posing for a death mask. She wore no makeup, and required none, for her high cheekbones had a warm natural coloring and her pleasingly pouted lips a pinkness of their own.

I felt a stirring in my crotch, a stirring that stiffened as I gazed along the length of her healthy, sculptured body, her succulent nipples, the ample curve of her hips, and her supine legs extending toward slender feet flawed only by skier's bunions on both her little toes. My hands were unsteady, damp, and I cursed myself: Cut it out, P. B.—this isn't very professional of you, old boy. All the same, my prick kept pressing against my fly. Now, nothing like this had so spontaneously happened to me before, though I'd massaged, and more than massaged, a fair share of arousing women—though none, admittedly, to compare with this Galatea. I wiped my wet hands against my trousers, and began to manipulate her neck and the upper regions of her shoulders, kneading the taut skin and tendons as though I were a merchant fingering costly fabric. At first she was tense, but gradually I induced suppleness, an easing.

"Hmm," she murmured, like a drowsy child. "That's nice. Tell me, how did you fall into the hands of our naughty Mr. Nelson?"

I was glad to talk; anything to get my mind off that mischievous hard-on. So not only did I tell her how I'd met Aces at a bar in Tangier, I continued with a brief resume of P. B. Jones and his journeys. A bastard, born in St. Louis and raised there in a Catholic orphanage until I was fifteen and ran away to Miami, where I'd worked as a masseur five or so years—until I'd saved enough money to go to New York and try my luck at what I really wanted to be, a writer. Successfully? Well, yes and no: I'd published a book of short stories—ignored, unfortunately, by both the critics and public, a disappointment that had brought me to Europe, and long years of traveling, scrounging about while I attempted to write a novel; but that, too, had been a dud. So here I was, still drifting and with no future that extended beyond tomorrow.

By now I'd reached her abdomen, massaged it with a rolling circular motion, then descended to her hips, and then, with my eyes on her rosy pubic hairs, I thought of Alice Lee Langman, and Alice Lee Langman's memories of a Polish lover who had enjoyed jamming her cunt with cherries and eating them out one by one. My imagination enhanced that fantasy. I imagined soft pitted cherries marinating in a bowl of warm rich sweetened cream, and I saw Kate McCloud's savory fingers selecting creamy cherries from the bowl and inserting them—My legs trembled, my cock pulsed, my balls were tight as a miser's fist. I said: "Excuse me," and walked into the bathroom, followed by Mutt, who watched with puzzled, pixie interest as I unzipped my fly and jacked off. It didn't take much: a couple of tugs and I launched a load that damn near flooded the floor. After removing the evidence with Kleenex, I washed my face, dried my hands, and returned to my client, my legs weak as a seasick sailor's but my cock still semi-saluting.

The dormer window was smudged with wintry Parisian dusk; lamplight defined her figure, silhouetted her face. She was smiling, and she said, a flickering amusement tempering her tone: "Feeling better?"

A bit gruffly, I said: "If you could turn over now . . . !"

I massaged the nape of her neck, rippled my fingers along her spine, and her torso vibrated, like a purring cat. "You know," she said, "I've thought of a name for your dog. Phoebe. I once had a pony named Phoebe. And a dog, too. But maybe we ought to ask Mutt. Mutt, how would you like to be called Phoebe?"

Mutt squatted to sprinkle the carpet.

"You see, she loves it! Mr. Jones," she said, "could I ask a great favor? Would you let Phoebe spend the night with me? I hate sleeping alone. And I've missed my other Phoebe so much."

"It's all right with me, if it's all right with . . . with Phoebe."

"Thank you" she said simply.

But it wasn't all right. I felt if I left Mutt here with this sorceress, she would never belong to me again. Or, perhaps, I'd never again belong to myself. It was as if I'd slipped into furious white water, an icy boiling current carrying me, slamming me toward some picturesque but dastardly cascade. Meanwhile my hands worked to soothe her back, buttocks, legs; her breathing became rhythmic and even. When I was sure she was asleep, I bent and kissed her ankle.

She moved, but did not waken. I sat down on the edge of the bed, and Phoebe—yes, *Phoebe*—jumped up and curled beside me; soon she was asleep herself. I had been loved, but I had never known love before, and so I could not comprehend the impulses, the desires careening around my brain like a bobsled. What could I do, what could I give Kate McCloud that would force her to respect and return my love? My eyes toured the room and settled on the fireplace mantel and the tables supporting the silver-framed picture of her child: such a serious little boy, though sometimes he was smiling, or lapping an ice-cream cone, or poking out his tongue and making comic faces. "Kidnap him"—wasn't that what the Black Duchess had advised? Absurd, but I saw myself, sword unsheathed, castrating dragons and fighting through infernos to rescue this child and bring him safely to his mother's arms. Pipe-dreams. Bullshit. And yet, instinct somehow told me the boy was the answer. Surreptitiously, I tiptoed out of the room and closed the door, disturbing neither Phoebe's slumbers nor those of her new mistress.

Time out. I need to sharpen pencils and begin a new notebook.

That was a long time out; almost a week. But it is November now, suddenly, unreasonably cold; I went out in a hard driving rain and caught a dandy. I wouldn't have gone out if my employer, Miss Victoria Self, the High Priestess of the Dial-A-Dick, Call-A-Cunt services, hadn't sent an urgent message ordering me to her office.

It beats me why, when you think of the money that woman must be coining, she and her Mafioso confederates, they can't fork out for slightly less sleazy headquarters than the two-room dump above a 42nd Street porno shop. Of course, the customers seldom see the premises; they only make contact by telephone. So I guess she figures why waste money pampering the help, us poor whores. Drowned, the rain water all but gushing out of my ears, I sloshed up the two flights of creaking stairs and once more confronted the frosted-glass door with chipped lettering: The Self Service. Walk In.

Four people occupied the stuffy little waiting room. Sal, a short hunky Italian wearing a wedding ring; he was one of Miss Self's moonlighting cops. And Andy, who was on probation for a burglary charge; but, if you didn't look too closely, he might pass for an average college-kid type; as usual, he was playing a harmonica. And then there was Butch, Miss Self's blond, languid secretary, who, now that the last of his Fire Island suntan had deserted him, resembled Uriah Heep more than ever. Maggie was there, too—a plump sweet girl: the last time I'd seen her she had just got married, greatly to Butch's indignation.

"And *now* guess what she's done!" Butch hissed as I walked in. "She's pregnant."

Maggie pleaded: "Please, Butch. I don't see why you're making such a hullabaloo. I only found out yesterday. It won't interfere."

"That's what you said when you sneaked off and married this bum. Maggie, you know I love you. But how could you have let such a thing happen?"

"Please, honey. I promise. It won't happen again."

Not mollified, but somewhat, Butch rustled papers on his desk and turned to Sal.

"Sal, I hope you're not forgetting you have a five o'clock appointment at the St. George hotel. Room 907. His name is Watson."

"The St. George! Jeez," grumbled Sal, whose nickname is Ten Penny because of his ability, when his dick is fully erect, to line ten pennies along its thick length, "that's in Brooklyn. I got to haul-ass way the hell over to Brooklyn in this weather?"

"It's a fifty-dollar date."

"I hope it's nothing fancy. I'm not up to anything fancy."

"Nothing fancy. Just a simple Golden Shower. The gentleman's thirsty."

"Well," said Sal, stepping over to a water cooler in the corner and grabbing himself a Dixie cup, "I guess I'd better tank up."

"Andy!"

"Yessir."

"Put that miserable harmonica in your pocket and leave it there."

"Yessir."

"Is that all you delinquents do in jail? Get yourselves tattooed and learn to play the harmonica."

"I ain't got any tattoo—"

"Don't talk back to me!"

"Yessir," said Andy humbly.

Butch swerved his attention my way; in his expression there was an extra-added smugness hinting that he might be privy to some ominous information concerning me. He pressed a buzzer on his desk, and said: "I believe Miss Self is ready to see you now."

Miss Self seemed oblivious to my entrance; she was stationed at a window, her back to me, pondering the downpour. Thin grey braids were looped around her narrow skull; as always, her stoutish figure bulged inside a blue serge suit. She was smoking a cigarillo. Her head swiveled. "Ah, so," she said with the leftover remnants of a German accent, "you are very wet. That is not good. Have you no raincoat?"

"I was hoping Santa Claus would bring me one for Christmas."

"That is not good," she repeated, advancing toward her desk. "You have been making good money. For sure you can afford a raincoat. Here," she said, producing from a drawer two glasses and a bottle of her preferred tranquilizer, tequila. While she poured, I wondered anew at the severity of the setting, starker than a penitent's cell, utterly unadorned except for the desk, some straight-back chairs, a Coca-Cola calendar, and a wall of filing cabinets (how I would have liked to have got a look inside those!). The only frivolous object in view was the gold Cartier watch flashing on Miss Self's wrist; it was so out of character. I puzzled as to how she had acquired it—was it perhaps a gift from one of her rich and grateful clients?

"Kicks", she said, emptying her glass with a shudder.

"Kicks."

"*Alors,*" she said, sucking her cigarillo, "you may recall our first interview. When you applied here as a potential employee of The Service. Recommended by Mr. Woodrow Hamilton—who, I regret to say, is no longer with us."

"Oh?"

"For a serious infraction of Our Rules. Which is precisely what I want to discuss with you." She narrowed her pale Teutonic eyes; I felt the queasiness of a captured soldier about to be interrogated by the Commandant of the Camp. "I acquainted you with those rules in complete detail; but to refresh your memory, I will remind you of the more important ones. Firstly, any attempt by a member of our staff to blackmail or embarrass a client will result in *severe* retribution."

A vision of a strangled corpse floating in the Harlem River insinuated itself.

"Secondly, under no circumstances will an employee ever deal directly with a client; all contacts, and all discussion of fees, must be made through our auspices. Thirdly, and most especially, an employee must never associate socially with a client: that sort of thing is not good business and can result in very disagreeable situations."

She doused her cigarillo in the tequila, and downed a generous slug straight from the bottle. "On September eleventh you had an appointment with a Mr. Appleton. You spent an hour with him in his room at the Yale Club. Did anything unusual happen?"

"Not really. It was just a one-way oral deal; he didn't want any reciprocation." I paused, but her unsatisfied demeanor indicated that she expected to hear more. "He was in his early sixties, but in good condition, hearty. A likable guy. Friendly. He talked a lot; he told me he was retired and lived on a farm with his second wife. He said he raised cattle—"

Miss Self impatiently interrupted: "And he gave you a hundred dollars."

"Yes."

"Did he give you anything else?"

I decided not to lie. "He gave me his calling card. He said that if I ever felt like breathing country air, I was welcome to visit him."

"What became of this card?"

"I threw it away. Lost it. I don't know."

She lit another cigarillo, and smoked it until a long ash tumbled off it. She picked up an envelope lying on her desk, extracted a letter from it, and spread it out before her. "I've worked more than twenty years in this business, but this morning I received a letter unique in my experience."

As I may have mentioned before, one of my gifts is an ability to read upside down: those of us who subsist on our wits develop offbeat talents. So, while Miss Self examined the mysterious communication, I read it. It said: *Dear Miss Self, I was well pleased with the amiable fellow you arranged to meet me at the Yale Club this past September 11th. So much so that I would like to get to know him better in a more gemütlich atmosphere. I wondered if it could be arranged, through your auspices, to have him spend the Thanksgiving holidays here at my farm in Pennsylvania? Say Thursday through Sunday. It would be a simple family gathering; my wife, some of my children, a few of my grandchildren. Naturally, I would expect to pay a reasonable fee, and I leave it to you to assess the amount. I trust this finds you well and in good spirit. Most sincerely, Roger W. Appleton.*

Miss Self read the letter aloud. "Now," she snapped, "what do you say to that?" When I did not readily reply, she said: "There's something wrong. Something suspicious. But putting that aside, it stands in contradiction to one of our primary rules: a Service employee must never associate socially with a client. These rules are not arbitrary. They are founded on experience." Frowning, she tapped the letter with a fingernail. "What do you suppose this man could have in mind? A *partouze?* Involving his wife?"

Careful to sound indifferent, I said: "I can't see any harm in that."

"Ah, so," she accused me. "You see nothing against this proposal? You *want* to go."

"Well, frankly, Miss Self, I'd welcome a change of scenery for a few days. I've had a pretty rough time this past year or so."

She slugged down another double dose of the cactus juice; shuddered. "Very well, I will write Mr. Appleton, and ask a fee of five hundred dollars. Perhaps, for a sum like that, we can for once overlook a rule. And with your share of the profits, promise me you'll buy a raincoat."

Aces waved to me as I entered the Ritz bar. It was six o'clock and I had to squeeze my way toward him between the populated tables, for at cocktail time the bar brimmed with suntanned skiers recently descended from Alpine holidays; and pairs of expensive tarts keeping each other company while waiting to be winked at by German and American businessmen; and battalions of fashion writers and Seventh Avenue rag traders gathered in Paris to view the summer collections; and of course, the chic old blue-haired ladies—there are always several of them, elderly permanent residents of the hotel, ensconced in the Ritz bar sipping their allotted two martinis ("my doctor insists: so good for the circulation") before retiring to the dining room to chew in mute chandeliered isolation.

I had no sooner sat down than Aces was summoned to answer a telephone call. I had a good view of him, for the telephone is located at the far end of the bar; occasionally his lips moved, but mostly he seemed to be just listening and nodding. Not that I was really watching him, for my mind was still upstairs contemplating Kate McCloud's loose hair, her dreaming head—a spectacle so consuming that Aces' return startled me.

"That was Kate," he announced, looking self-satisfied: a mongoose digesting a mouse. "She wanted to know why you left without saying good-bye."

"She was asleep."

Aces always carries a mess of kitchen matches in a jacket pocket, it's one of his affectations; he lighted one with his thumbnail and touched the flame to a cigarette. "She may not seem so, but Kate's a very knowledgeable young woman—her instincts are usually sound. She liked you very much. And so," he said, grinning, "I'm in a position to make you a solid offer. Kate would like to hire you as a paid companion. You will receive a thousand dollars a month and all your expenses, including clothing and your own car."

I said: "Why did she marry Axel Jaeger?"

Aces blinked, as if this was the last reaction he had expected from me. He stalled. Then: "Perhaps a more interesting question would be—why did *he* marry her? And an even more interesting question is—how did Kate meet him? You see, Axel Jaeger is an elusive man. I've never encountered him myself, only seen *paparazzi* photographs: a tall man with a Heidelberg sword-scar across his cheek, thin, almost emaciated, a man in his late fifties. He comes from Dusseldorf, and inherited an ammunitions fortune from his grandfather, a fortune he has astronomically increased. He has factories all over Germany, all over the world—he owns oil tankers, oil fields in Texas and Alaska, he has the largest cattle ranch in Brazil, over eight hundred square miles, and a fair share of both Ireland and Switzerland (all the rich West Germans have been buying up Ireland and Switzerland: they think they'll be safe there if the bombs start falling again). Jaeger is easily the richest man in Germany—and possibly Europe. He's a German national, but he has a permanent Swiss residence permit; for tax reasons, naturally. To keep it, he has to spend six months of the year in Switzerland whether he likes it or not. God, what tortures the rich won't endure to protect a penny. He lives in a colossal, and colossally ugly, château on a mountainside about three miles north of St. Moritz. I don't know anyone who has ever been inside the place. Except Kate, of course.

"As I understand it, he was, and is, a very convinced Catholic. And for that reason he remained married to his first wife for twenty-seven loyal years, or until she died. Even though she was unable to give him a child, which seems to have been the crux of the matter, for he wanted a child, a son, to continue the Jaeger dynasty. That being the case, why didn't he do the obvious and marry a well-bred, wide-hipped German girl who could fill up a nursery bim-bam? Certainly a clever soigné beauty like Kate would hardly seem the ideal choice for a man of Herr Jaeger's constrained austerity. And, so far as that goes, it's incomprehensible that Kate would find herself attracted to such a person. Money? That couldn't have been as issue. Actually, after I first really got to know Kate, she told me that her first marriage had been such a trauma, she never intended to marry again. And yet, within a few months, and without any signal, without ever mentioning that she even knew this legendary tycoon, she obtained a papal annulment from her first marriage and marries Jaeger in a Catholic ceremony at the Dusseldorf Cathedral. One year later the prayed-for heir arrives. Heinrich Rheinhardt Jaeger. Heinie. And a year after that, less than a year, she seems to have been dismissed from the Jaeger château, luggage et al., leaving the boy in the father's custody—though granted certain highly limited visiting privileges."

"But you don't know why?"

Aces thumbnailed another kitchen match, and blew it out. "The fall-out, or whatever one may call it, was as enigmatic as the alliance itself. She disappeared for several months, and a doctor I know told me she had spent them cloistered at the Nestlé Clinic in Lausanne. But as for what happened, she's not confided in me, and I've never had the courage to inquire. I suppose the only person who really knows is Kate's maid, Corinne. And when it comes to Miss Kate, Corinne is as close-mouthed as an Easter Island monument."

"Well. But why didn't they get a divorce?"

"The Catholic hang-up, I suppose. He would never countenance divorce."

"For Christ sake, she could divorce him, couldn't she?"

"Not if she ever wanted to see Heinie again. That door would be shut forever."

"Sonofabitch. I'd like to shove a shotgun up his ass and pull the trigger. Bastard. But you mentioned danger. I can't see where she has anything to be afraid of."

"Kate thinks she does. So do I. And it isn't any paranoid fantasy that Jaeger has agents following her, or gathering information on her wherever she goes, whatever she does. If she changes a Kotex, you can be sure the *Grand Seigneur* hears about it. Look," he said, snapping his fingers for a waiter "let's have a drink. It's too late for daiquiris. How about a Scotch-soda?"

"I don't care."

"Waiter, two Scotch-soda. Now, as to this offer I've made you —are the terms satisfactory, or would you like a few days to think it over?"

"I don't have to think it over. I've already decided."

The drinks arrived, and he lifted his glass. "Then we'll drink to your decision, whatever it is. Though I hope it's yes."

"Yes."

He relaxed. "You're a godsend, P. B. And I'm sure you'll not regret it." Seldom has a more untrue prophecy been prophesied.

"Yes, it's yes. But. If he doesn't want a divorce, what *does* he want?"

"I have a theory. It's only a theory, but I'd bet my last chip that it's accurate. He intends to kill her." Aces tinkled the ice in his glass. "Since the strictness of his Catholicism forbids divorce, and because as long as she's alive she represents a threat to him, a threat to him and the custody of his child. So he means to kill her. Murder her in a manner that will look like an accident."

"Aces. Oh, come on. You're crazy. Either you're crazy. Or he is."

"On this particular subject, yes, I believe he is crazy. Hey," he said, "I just noticed something. Where's your dog?"

"I gave her to the lady upstairs."

"Well, well, *well.* I can see you really were quite impressed."

I walked all the way home from the Proustian-ghosted corridors of the Ritz to the rickety rat-trap halls of my hotel near the Gare du Nord. An elation lightened the journey—at last I wasn't a deadbeat expatriate, an aimless loser; I was a man with a mission in life, an *assignment;* and like some cub scout about to embark on his first overnight hike, my mind childishly churned with preparations. Clothes; I would need shirts, shoes, some good new suits, for nothing in my wardrobe would survive scrutiny in strong sunlight. And a weapon; tomorrow I would buy a .38 revolver and start practice at a shooting range. I walked fast, not simply because it was cold with that Seine-damp misty coldness peculiar to Paris, but because I hoped the exercise would so exhaust me that I would fall into dreamless sleep as soon as I put my head against a pillow. And I did.

But it was not a dreamless sleep. I well understand why analysts demand high payment, for what can be more tedious than listening to another person recount his dreams? But I'll chance boring you with the dream I dreamt that night, because in future time it came to be realized in almost every detail. In the beginning the dream was motionless, a seaside scene like a Boudin painting at the turn of the century. Still figures on a vast beach with an aquamarine sea just beyond them. A man, a woman, a dog, a young boy. The woman is wearing an ankle-length taffeta dress —sea breezes seem to be teasing its skirt; and she is carrying a green parasol. The man sports a straw boater; the boy is outfitted in a sailor suit. Eventually the picture comes into much closer focus, and I recognize the woman under the parasol—she's Kate McCloud. And the man, who now reaches to hold her hand, is myself. Suddenly the sailor-suited child seizes a stick and throws it into the waves; the dog rushes to retrieve it, and races back, shaking itself and shimmering the air with crystals of sea water.

III

LA CÔTE BASQUE

*O*verheard in a cowboy bar in Roswell, New Mexico
. . . FIRST COWBOY: Hey, Jed. How are you? How you feeling?
SECOND COWBOY: Good! Real good. I feel so good I didn't have
to jack off this morning to get my heart started.

"*Carissimo!*" she cried. "You're just what I'm looking for. A
lunch date. The duchess stood me up."

"Black or white?" I said.

"White," she said, reversing my direction on the sidewalk.

White is Wallis Windsor, whereas the Black Duchess is what
her friends call Perla Apfeldorf, the Brazilian wife of a notori-
ously racist South African diamond industrialist. As for the lady
who also knew the distinction, she was indeed a lady—Lady Ina
Coolbirth, an American married to a British chemicals tycoon
and a lot of woman in every way. Tall, taller than most men,

Ina was a big breezy peppy broad, born and raised on a ranch in Montana.

"This is the second time she's canceled," Ina Coolbirth continued. "She says she has hives. Or the duke has hives. One or the other. Anyway, I've still got a table at Côte Basque. So, shall we? Because I do so need someone to talk to, really. And, thank God, Jonesy, it can be you."

Côte Basque is on East Fifty-fifth Street, directly across from the St. Regis. It was the site of the original Le Pavillon, founded in 1940 by the honorable restaurateur Henri Soulé. M. Soulé abandoned the premises because of a feud with his landlord, the late president of Columbia Pictures, a sleazy Hollywood hood named Harry Cohn (who, upon learning that Sammy Davis, Jr., was "dating" his blond star Kim Novak, ordered a hit man to call Davis and tell him: "Listen, Sambo, you're already missing one eye. How'd you like to try for none?" The next day Davis married a Las Vegas chorus girl—colored). Like Côte Basque, the original Pavillon consisted of a small entrance area, a bar to the left of this, and in the rear, through an archway, a large red-plush dining room. The bar and main room formed an Outer Hebrides, an Elba to which Soulé exiled second-class patrons. Preferred clients, selected by the proprietor with unerring *snobbisme,* were placed in the banquette-lined entrance area—a practice pursued by every New York restaurant of established chic: Lafayette, The Colony, La Grenouille, La Caravelle. These tables, always nearest the door, are drafty, afford the least privacy, but nevertheless, to be seated at one, or not, is a status-sensitive citizen's moment of truth. Harry Cohn never made it at Pavillon. It didn't matter that he was a hotshot Hollywood hottentot or even that he was Soulé's landlord. Soulé saw him for the shoulder-padded counter-jumper Cohn was and accordingly ushered him to a table in the sub-zero regions of the rear room. Cohn cursed, he huffed, puffed, revenged himself by upping and upping the restaurant's rent. So Soulé simply moved to more regal quarters in the Ritz Tower. However, while Soulé was still settling there, Harry Cohn cooled (Jerry Wald, when asked why he attended the funeral, replied: "Just to be sure the bastard was dead"), and Soulé, nostalgic for his old stamping ground, again leased the address from the new custodians and created, as a second enterprise, a sort of boutique variation on Le Pavillon: La Côte Basque.

Lady Ina, of course, was allotted an impeccable position—the fourth table on the left as you enter. She was escorted to it by none other than M. Soulé, distrait as ever, pink and glazed as a marzipan pig.

"Lady Coolbirth . . ." he muttered, his perfectionist eyes spinning about in search of cankered roses and awkward waiters. "Lady Coolbirth . . . umn . . . very nice . . . umn . . . and Lord Coolbirth? . . . umn . . . today we have on the wagon a very nice saddle of lamb . . ."

She consulted me, a glance, and said: "I think not anything off the wagon. It arrives too quickly. Let's have something that takes forever. So that we can get drunk and disorderly. Say a soufflé Furstenberg. Could you do that, Monsieur Soulé?"

He tutted his tongue—on two counts: he disapproves of customers dulling their taste buds with alcohol, and also: "Furstenberg is a great nuisance. An uproar."

Delicious, though: a froth of cheese and spinach into which an assortment of poached eggs has been sunk strategically, so that, when struck by your fork, the soufflé is moistened with golden rivers of egg yolk.

"An uproar," said Ina, "is exactly what I want," and the proprietor, touching his sweat-littered forehead with a bit of handkerchief, acquiesced.

Then she decided against cocktails, saying: "Why not have a proper reunion?" From the wine steward she ordered a bottle of Roederer's Cristal. Even for those who dislike champagne, myself among them, there are two champagnes one can't refuse: Dom Pérignon and the even superior Cristal, which is bottled in a natural-colored glass that displays its pale blaze, a chilled fire of such prickly dryness that, swallowed, seems not to have been swallowed at all, but instead to have turned to vapors on the tongue and burned there to one damp sweet ash.

"Of course," said Ina, "champagne does have one serious drawback: swilled as a regular thing, a certain sourness settles in the tummy, and the result is permanent bad breath. Really incurable. Remember Arturo's breath, bless his heart? And Cole adored champagne. God, I do miss Cole so, dotty as he was those last years. Did I ever tell you the story about Cole and the stud wine steward? I can't remember quite where he worked. He was Italian, so it couldn't have been here or Pav. The Colony? Odd: I see him clearly—a nut-brown man, beautifully flat, with oiled hair and the sexiest jawline—but I can't see *where* I see him. He was a southern Italian, so they called him Dixie, and Teddie Whitestone got knocked up by him—Bill Whitestone aborted her himself under the impression it was his doing. And perhaps it was—in quite another context—but still I think it rather dowdy, unnatural, if you will, a doctor aborting his own wife. Teddie Whitestone wasn't alone; there was a queue of gals greasing Dixie's palm with billetsdoux. Cole's approach was creative: he invited Dixie to his apartment under the pretext of getting advice on the laying in of a new wine cellar—Cole! who knew more about wine than that dago ever dreamed. So they were sitting there on the couch —the lovely suede one Billy Baldwin made for Cole—all very informal, and Cole kisses this fellow on the cheek, and Dixie grins and says: 'That will cost you five hundred dollars, Mr. Porter.' Cole just laughs and squeezes Dixie's leg. 'Now that will cost you a thousand dollars, Mr. Porter.' Then Cole realized this piece of pizza was serious; and so he unzipped him, hauled it out, shook it, and said: 'What will be the full price on the use of that?' Dixie told him two thousand dollars. Cole went straight to his desk, wrote a check and handed it to him. And he said: 'Miss Otis regrets she's unable to lunch today. Now get out.'"

·   ·   ·

The Cristal was being poured. Ina tasted it. "It's not cold enough. But ahhh!" She swallowed again. "I do miss Cole. And Howard Sturgis. Even Papa; after all, he did write about me in *Green Hills of Africa*. And Uncle Willie. Last week in London I went to a party at Drue Heinz's and got stuck with Princess Margaret. Her mother's a darling, but the rest of that family!— though Prince Charles may amount to something. But basically, royals think there are just three categories: colored folk, white folk, and royals. Well, I was about to doze off, she's such a drone, when suddenly she announced, apropos of nothing, that she had decided she really didn't like 'poufs'! An extraordinary remark, source considered. Remember the joke about who got the first sailor? But I simply lowered my eyes, *très* Jane Austen, and said: 'In that event, ma'am, I fear you will spend a very lonely old age.' Her expression!—I thought she might turn me into a pumpkin."

There was an uncharacteristic bite and leap to Ina's voice, as though she were speeding along helter-skelter to avoid confiding what it was she wanted, but didn't want, to confide. My eyes and ears were drifting elsewhere. The occupants of a table placed catty-corner to ours were two people I'd met together in South-ampton last summer, though the meeting was not of such import that I expected them to recognize me—Gloria Vanderbilt de Cicco Stokowski Lumet Cooper and her childhood chum Carol Marcus Saroyan Saroyan (she married *him* twice) Matthau: women in their late thirties, but looking not much removed from those deb days when they were grabbing Lucky Balloons at the Stork Club.

"But what can you say," inquired Mrs. Matthau of Mrs. Cooper, "to someone who's lost a good lover, weighs two hundred pounds, and is in the dead center of a nervous collapse? I don't think she's been out of bed for a month. Or changed the sheets. 'Maureen'—this is what I *did* tell her—'Maureen, I've been in a lot worse condition than you. I remember once when I was going around stealing sleeping pills out of other people's medicine cabinets, saving up to bump myself off. I was in debt up to here, every penny I had was borrowed . . .' "

"*Dar*ling," Mrs. Cooper protested with a tiny stammer, "why didn't you come to *me?*"

"Because you're rich. It's much less difficult to borrow from the poor."

"But, *dar*ling . . ."

Mrs. Matthau proceeded. "So I said: 'Do you know what I did, Maureen? Broke as I was, I went out and hired myself a *personal* maid. My fortunes rose, my outlook changed completely, I felt loved and pampered. So if I were you, Maureen, I'd go into hock and hire some very expensive creature to run my bath and turn down the bed.' Incidentally, did you go to the Logans' party?"

"For an hour."

"How was it?"

"Marvelous. If you've never been to a party before."

145

"I wanted to go. But you know Walter. I never imagined I'd marry an actor. Well, *marry* perhaps. But not for love. Yet here I've been stuck with Walter all these years and it still makes me curdle if I see his eye stray a fraction. Have you seen this new Swedish cunt called Karen something?"

"Wasn't she in some spy picture?"

"Exactly. Lovely face. Divine photographed from the bazooms up. But the legs are strictly redwood forest. Absolute tree trunks. Anyway, we met her at the Widmarks' and she was moving her eyes around and making all these little noises for Walter's benefit, and I stood it as long as I could, but when I heard Walter say 'How old are you, Karen?' I said 'For God's sake, Walter, why don't you chop off her legs and read the rings?' "

"Carol! You didn't."

"You know you can always count on me."

"And she heard you?"

"It wouldn't have been very interesting if she hadn't."

Mrs. Matthau extracted a comb from her purse and began drawing it through her long albino hair: another leftover from her World War II debutante nights—an era when she and all her *compères*, Gloria and Honeychile and Oona and Jinx, slouched against El Morocco upholstery ceaselessly raking their Veronica Lake locks.

"I had a letter from Oona this morning," Mrs. Matthau said.

"So did I," Mrs. Cooper said.

"Then you know they're having another baby."

"Well, I assumed so. I always do."

"That Charlie is a lucky bastard," said Mrs. Matthau.

"Of course, Oona would have made any man a great wife."

"Nonsense. With Oona, only geniuses need apply. Before she met Charlie, she wanted to marry Orson Welles . . . and she wasn't even seventeen. It was Orson who introduced her to Charlie; he said: 'I know just the guy for you. He's rich, he's a genius, and there's nothing that he likes more than a dutiful young daughter.' "

Mrs. Cooper was thoughtful. "If Oona hadn't married Charlie, I don't suppose I would have married Leopold."

"And if Oona hadn't married Charlie, and you hadn't married Leopold, I wouldn't have married Bill Saroyan. Twice yet."

The two women laughed together, their laughter like a naughty but delightfully sung duet. Though they were not physically similar—Mrs. Matthau being blonder than Harlow and as lushly white as a gardenia, while the other had brandy eyes and a dark dimpled brilliance markedly present when her negroid lips flashed smiles—one sensed they were two of a kind: charmingly incompetent adventuresses.

Mrs. Matthau said: "Remember the Salinger thing?"

"Salinger?"

"*A Perfect Day for Banana Fish.* That Salinger."

"*Franny and Zooey.*"

"Umn huh. You don't remember about him?"

Mrs. Cooper pondered, pouted; no, she didn't.

"It was while we were still at Brearley," said Mrs. Matthau. "Before Oona met Orson. She had a mysterious beau, this Jewish boy with a Park Avenue mother, Jerry Salinger. He wanted to be a writer, and he wrote Oona letters ten pages long while he was overseas in the army. Sort of love-letter essays, very tender, tenderer than God. Which is a bit too tender. Oona used to read them to me, and when she asked what I thought, I said it seemed to me he must be a boy who cries very easily; but what she wanted to know was whether I thought he was brilliant and talented or really just silly, and I said both, he's both, and years later when I read *Catcher in the Rye* and realized the author was Oona's Jerry, I was still inclined to that opinion."

"I never heard a strange story about Salinger," Mrs. Cooper confided.

"I've never heard anything about him that wasn't strange. He's certainly not your normal everyday Jewish boy from Park Avenue."

"Well, it isn't really about *him*, but about a friend of his who went to visit him in New Hampshire. He does live there, doesn't he? On some very remote farm? Well, it was February and terribly cold. One morning Salinger's friend was missing. He wasn't in his bedroom or anywhere around the house. They found him finally, deep in a snowy woods. He was lying in the snow wrapped in a blanket and holding an empty whiskey bottle. He'd killed himself by drinking the whiskey until he'd fallen asleep and frozen to death."

After a while Mrs. Matthau said: "That *is* a strange story. It must have been lovely, though—all warm with whiskey, drifting off into the cold starry air. Why did he do it?"

"All I know is what I told you," Mrs. Cooper said.

An exiting customer, a florid-at-the-edges swarthy balding Charlie sort of fellow, stopped at their table. He fixed on Mrs. Cooper a gaze that was intrigued, amused and . . . a trifle grim. He said: "Hello, Gloria"; and she smiled: "Hello, darling"; but her eyelids twitched as she attempted to identify him; and then he said: "Hello, Carol. How are ya, doll?" and she knew who he was all right: "Hello, darling. Still living in Spain?" He nodded; his glance returned to Mrs. Cooper: "Gloria, you're as beautiful as ever. More beautiful. See ya . . ." He waved and walked away.

Mrs. Cooper stared after him, scowling.

Eventually Mrs. Matthau said: "You didn't recognize him, did you?"

"N-n-no."

"Life. Life. Really, it's too sad. There was nothing familiar about him at all?"

"Long ago. Something. A dream."

"It wasn't a dream."

"Carol. Stop that. Who is he?"

"Once upon a time you thought very highly of him. You cooked his meals and washed his socks"—Mrs. Cooper's eyes enlarged, shifted—"and when he was in the army you followed him from camp to camp, living in dreary furnished rooms—"

3

"No!"

"Yes!"

"No."

"Yes, Gloria. Your first husband."

"That . . . man . . . was . . . Pat di Cicco?"

"Oh, darling. Let's not brood. After all, you haven't seen him in almost twenty years. You were only a child. Isn't that," said Mrs. Matthau, offering a diversion, "Jackie Kennedy?"

And I heard Lady Ina on the subject, too: "I'm almost blind with these specs, but just coming in there, isn't that Mrs. Kennedy? And her sister?"

It was; I knew the sister because she had gone to school with Kate McCloud, and when Kate and I were on Abner Dustin's yacht at the Feria in Seville she had lunched with us, then afterward we'd gone water-skiing together, and I've often thought of it, how perfect she was, a gleaming gold-brown girl in a white bathing suit, her white skis hissing smoothly, her brown-gold hair whipping as she swooped and skidded between the waves. So it was pleasant when she stopped to greet Lady Ina ("Did you know I was on the plane with you from London? But you were sleeping so nicely I didn't dare speak") and seeing me, remembered me: "Why, hello there, Jonesy," she said, her rough whispery warm voice very slightly vibrating her, "how's your sunburn? Remember, I warned you, but you wouldn't listen." Her laughter trailed off as she folded herself onto a banquette beside her sister, their heads inclining toward each other in whispering Bouvier conspiracy. It was puzzling how much they resembled one another without sharing any common feature beyond identical voices and wide-apart eyes and certain gestures, particularly a habit of staring deeply into an interlocutor's eyes while ceaselessly nodding the head with a mesmerizingly solemn sympathy.

Lady Ina observed: "You can see those girls have swung a few big deals in their time. I know many people can't abide either of them, usually women, and I can understand that, because they don't like women and almost never have anything good to say about *any* woman. But they're perfect with men, a pair of Western geisha girls; they know how to keep a man's secrets and how to make him feel important. If I were a man, I'd fall for Lee myself. She's marvelously made, like a Tanagra figurine; she's feminine without being effeminate; and she's one of the few people I've known who can be both candid and cozy—ordinarily one cancels the other. Jackie—no, not on the same planet. Very photogenic, of course; but the effect is a little . . . unrefined, exaggerated."

I thought of an evening when I'd gone with Kate McCloud and a gang to a drag-queen contest held in a Harlem ballroom: hundreds of young queens sashaying in hand-sewn gowns to the funky honking of saxophones: Brooklyn supermarket clerks, Wall Street runners, black dishwashers, and Puerto Rican waiters adrift in silk and fantasy, chorus boys and bank cashiers and Irish elevator boys got up as Marilyn Monroe, as Audrey Hepburn, as Jackie

Kennedy. Indeed, Mrs. Kennedy was the most popular inspiration; a dozen boys, the winner among them, wore her high-rise hairdo, winged eyebrows, sulky, palely painted mouth. And, in life, that is how she struck me—not as a bona fide woman, but as an artful female impersonator impersonating Mrs. Kennedy.

I explained what I was thinking to Ina, and she said: "That's what I meant by . . . exaggerated." Then: "Did you ever know Rosita Winston? Nice woman. Half Cherokee, I believe. She had a stroke some years ago, and now she can't speak. Or, rather, she can say just one word. That very often happens after a stroke, one's left with one word out of all the words one has known. Rosita's word is 'beautiful.' Very appropriate, since Rosita has always loved beautiful things. What reminded me of it was old Joe Kennedy. He, too, has been left with one word. And his word is: 'Goddammit!' " Ina motioned the waiter to pour champagne. "Have I ever told you about the time he assaulted me? When I was eighteen and a guest in his house, a friend of his daughter Kek . . ."

Again, my eye coasted the length of the room, catching, *en passant*, a bluebearded Seventh Avenue brassiere hustler trying to con a closet-queen editor from *The New York Times*; and Diana Vreeland, the pomaded, peacock-iridescent editor of *Vogue*, sharing a table with an elderly man who suggested a precious object of discreet *extravagance*, perhaps a fine grey pearl—Mainbocher; and Mrs. William S. Paley lunching with her sister, Mrs. John Hay Whitney. Seated near them was a pair unknown to me: a woman forty, forty-five, no beauty but very handsomely set up inside a brown Balenciaga suit with a brooch composed of cinnamon-colored diamonds fixed to the lapel. Her companion was much younger, twenty, twenty-two, a hearty sun-browned statue who looked as if he might have spent the summer sailing alone across the Atlantic. Her son? But no, because . . . he lit a cigarette and passed it to her and their fingers touched significantly; then they were holding hands.

". . . the old bugger slipped into my bedroom. It was about six o'clock in the morning, the ideal hour if you want to catch someone really slugged out, really by complete surprise, and when I woke up he was already between the sheets with one hand over my mouth and the other all over the place. The sheer ballsy gall of it—right there in his own house with the whole family sleeping all around us. But all those Kennedy men are the same; they're like dogs, they have to pee on every fire hydrant. Still, you had to give the old guy credit, and when he saw I wasn't going to scream he was *so* grateful . . ."

But they were not conversing, the older woman and the young seafarer; they held hands, and then he smiled and presently she smiled, too.

"Afterward—can you imagine?—he pretended nothing had happened, there was never a wink or a nod, just the good old daddy of my schoolgirl chum. It was uncanny and rather cruel; after all, he'd had me and I'd even pretended to enjoy it: there should have been some sentimental acknowledgment, a bauble, a cigarette box . . ." She sensed my other interest, and her eyes strayed to the improbable lovers. She said: "Do you know that story?"

"No," I said. "But I can see there has to be one."

"Though it's not what you think. Uncle Willie could have made something divine out of it. So could Henry James—better than Uncle Willie, because Uncle Willie would have cheated, and for the sake of a movie sale, would have made Delphine and Bobby lovers."

Delphine Austin from Detroit; I'd read about her in the columns—an heiress married to a marbleized pillar of New York clubman society. Bobby, her companion, was Jewish, the son of hotel magnate S. L. L. Semenenko and first husband of a weird young movie cutie who had divorced him to marry his father (and whom the father had divorced when he caught her in flagrante with a German shepherd . . . dog. I'm not kidding).

According to Lady Ina, Delphine Austin and Bobby Semenenko had been inseparable the past year or so, lunching every day at Côte Basque and Lutèce and L'Aiglon, traveling in winter to Gstaad and Lyford Cay, skiing, swimming, spreading themselves with utmost vigor considering the bond was not June-and-January frivolities but really the basis for a double-bill, double-barreled, three-handkerchief variation on an old Bette Davis weeper like *Dark Victory:* they both were dying of leukemia.

"I mean, a worldly woman and a beautiful young man who

travel together with death as their common lover and companion. Don't you think Henry James could have done something with that? Or Uncle Willie?"

"No. It's too corny for James, and not corny enough for Maugham."

"Well, you must admit, Mrs. Hopkins would make a fine tale."

"Who?" I said.

"Standing there," Ina Coolbirth said.

That Mrs. Hopkins. A redhead dressed in black; black hat with a veil trim, a black Mainbocher suit, black crocodile purse, crocodile shoes. M. Soulé had an ear cocked as she stood whispering to him; and suddenly everyone was whispering. Mrs. Kennedy and her sister had elicited not a murmur, nor had the entrances of Lauren Bacall and Katharine Cornell and Clare Boothe Luce. However, Mrs. Hopkins was *une autre chose:* a sensation to unsettle the suavest Côte Basque client. There was nothing surreptitious in the attention allotted her as she moved with head bowed toward a table where an escort already awaited her—a Catholic priest, one of those highbrow, malnutritional, Father D'Arcy clerics who always seems most at home when absent from the cloisters and while consorting with the very grand and very rich in a wine-and-roses stratosphere.

"Only," said Lady Ina, "Ann Hopkins would think of that. To advertise your search for spiritual 'advice' in the most public possible manner. Once a tramp, always a tramp."

"You don't think it was an accident?" I said.

"Come out of the trenches, boy. The war's over. Of course it wasn't an accident. She killed David with malice aforethought. She's a murderess. The police know that."

"Then how did she get away with it?"

"Because the family wanted her to. David's family. And, as it happened in Newport, old Mrs. Hopkins had the power to prevail. Have you ever met David's mother? Hilda Hopkins?"

"I saw her once last summer in Southampton. She was buying a pair of tennis shoes. I wondered what a woman her age, she must be eighty, wanted with tennis shoes. She looked like . . . some very old goddess."

"She is. That's why Ann Hopkins got away with cold-blooded murder. Her mother-in-law is a Rhode Island goddess. *And* a saint."

Ann Hopkins had lifted her veil and was now whispering to the priest, who, servilely entranced, was brushing a Gibson against his starved blue lips.

"But it *could* have been an accident. If one goes by the papers. As I remember, they'd just come home from a dinner party in Watch Hill and gone to bed in separate rooms. Weren't there supposed to have been a recent series of burglaries thereabouts? —and she kept a shotgun by her bed, and suddenly in the dark her bedroom door opened and she grabbed the shotgun and shot at what she thought was a prowler. Only it was her husband. David Hopkins. With a hole through his head."

"That's what she said. That's what her lawyer said. That's what the police said. And that's what the papers said . . . even the *Times*. But that isn't what happened." And Ina, inhaling like a skin diver, began: "Once upon a time a jazzy little carrot-top killer rolled into town from Wheeling or Logan—somewhere in West Virginia. She was eighteen, she'd been brought up in some country-slum way, and she had already been married and divorced; or she *said* she'd been married a month or two to a marine and divorced him when he disappeared (keep that in mind: it's an important clue). Her name was Ann Cutler, and she looked rather like a malicious Betty Grable. She worked as a call girl for a pimp who was a bell captain at the Waldorf; and she saved her money and took voice lessons and dance lessons and ended up as the favorite lay of one of Frankie Costello's shysters, and he always took her to El Morocco. It was during the war—1943—and Elmer's was always full of gangsters and military brass. But one night an ordinary young marine showed up there; except that he wasn't ordinary: his father was one of the stuffiest men in the East—and richest. David had sweetness and great good looks, but he was just like old Mr. Hopkins really—an anal-oriented Episcopalian. Stingy. Sober. Not at all café society. But there he was at Elmer's, a soldier on leave, horny, and a bit stoned. One of Winchell's stooges was there, and he recognized the Hopkins boy; he bought David a drink, and said he could fix it up for him with any one of the girls he saw, just pick one, and David, poor sod, said the redhead with the button nose and big tits was okay by him. So the Winchell stooge sends her a note, and at dawn little David finds himself writhing inside the grip of an expert Cleopatra's clutch.

"I'm sure it was David's first experience with anything less primitive than a belly rub with his prep-school roomie. He went bonkers, not that one can blame him; I know some very grown-up Mr. Cool Balls who've gone bonkers over Ann Hopkins. She was clever with David; she knew she'd hooked a biggie, even if he was only a kid, so she quit what she was doing and got a job in lingerie at Saks; she never pressed for anything, refused any gift fancier than a handbag, and all the while he was in the service she wrote him every day, little letters cozy and innocent as a baby's layette. In fact, she *was* knocked up; and it *was* his kid; but she didn't tell him a thing until he next came home on leave and found his girl four months pregnant. Now, here is where she showed that certain venomous *élan* that separates truly dangerous serpents from mere chicken snakes: she told him she didn't want to marry him. Wouldn't marry him under any circumstances because she had no desire to lead a Hopkins life; she had neither the background nor innate ability to cope with it, and she was sure neither his family nor friends would ever accept her. She said all she would ever ask would be a modest amount of child support. David protested, but of course he was relieved, even though he would still have to go to his father with the story—David had no money of his own.

"It was then that Ann made her smartest move; she had been doing her homework, and she knew everything there was to know about David's parents; so she said: 'David, there's just one thing I'd like. I want to meet your family. I never had much family of my own, and I'd like my child to have some occasional contact with his grandparents. They might like that, too.' *C'est très joli, très diabolique, non?* And it worked. Not that Mr. Hopkins was fooled. Right from the start he said the girl was a tramp, and she would never see a nickel of his; but Hilda Hopkins fell for it —she believed that gorgeous hair and those blue malarkey eyes, the whole poor-little-match-girl pitch Ann was tossing her. And as David was the oldest son, and she was in a hurry for a grand-child, she did exactly what Ann had gambled on: she persuaded David to marry her, and her husband to, if not condone it, at least not forbid it. And for some while it seemed as if Mrs. Hopkins had been very wise: each year she was rewarded with another grandchild until there were three, two girls and a boy; and Ann's social pickup was incredibly quick—she crashed right through, not bothering to observe any speed limits. She certainly grasped the essentials, I'll say that. She learned to ride and became the horsiest horse-hag in Newport. She studied French and had a French butler and campaigned for the Best Dressed List by lunch-ing with Eleanor Lambert and inviting her for weekends. She learned about furniture and fabrics from Sister Parish and Billy Baldwin; and little Henry Geldzahler was pleased to come to tea (Tea! Ann Cutler! My God!) and to talk to her about modern paintings.

"But the deciding element in her success, leaving aside the fact she'd married a great Newport name, was the duchess. Ann realized something that only the cleverest social climbers ever do. If you want to ride swiftly and safely from the depths to the surface, the surest way is to single out a shark and attach yourself to it like a pilot fish. This is as true in Keokuk, where one massages, say, the local Mrs. Ford Dealer, as it is in Detroit, where you may as well try for Mrs. Ford herself—or in Paris or Rome. But why should Ann Hopkins, being by marriage a Hopkins and the daughter-in-law of *the* Hilda Hopkins, need the duchess? Because she needed the blessing of someone with presumably high standards, someone with international impact whose acceptance of her would silence the laughing hyenas. And who better than the duchess? As for the duchess, she has high tolerance for the flattery of rich ladies-in-waiting, the kind who always pick up the check; I wonder if the duchess has *ever* picked up a check. Not that it matters. She gives good value. She's one of that unusual female breed who are able to have a genuine friendship with another woman. Certainly she was a marvelous friend to Ann Hopkins. Of course, she wasn't taken in by Ann—after all, the duchess is too much of a con artist not to twig another one; but the idea amused her of taking this cool-eyed cardplayer and lacquering her with a little real style, launching her on the circuit, and the young Mrs. Hopkins became quite notorious—though without the style. The father of the second Hopkins girl was Fon Portago, or so everyone says, and God knows she does look very *espagnole;* however that may be, Ann Hopkins was definitely racing her motor in the Grand Prix manner.

"One summer she and David took a house at Cap Ferrat (she was trying to worm her way in with Uncle Willie: she even learned to play first-class bridge; but Uncle Willie said that while she was a woman he might enjoy writing about, she was not someone he trusted to have at his card table), and from Nice to Monte she was known by every male past puberty as Madame Marmalade—her favorite *petit déjeuner* being hot cock buttered with Dundee's best. Although I'm told it's actually strawberry jam she prefers. I don't think David guessed the full measure of these fandangos, but there was no doubt he was miserable, and after a while he fell in with the very girl he ought to have married originally—his second cousin, Mary Kendall, no beauty but a sensible, attractive girl who had always been in love with him. She was engaged to Tommy Bedford but broke it off when David asked her to marry him. *If* he could get a divorce. And he *could;* all it would cost him, according to Ann, was five million dollars tax-free. David still had no glue of his own, and when he took this proposition to his father, Mr. Hopkins said *never!* and said he'd always warned that Ann was what she was, bad baggage, but David hadn't listened, so now that was his burden, and as long as the father lived she would never get a subway token. After this, David hired a detective and within six months had enough evidence, including Polaroids of her being screwed front and back by a couple of jockeys in Saratoga, to have her jailed, much less divorce her. But when David confronted her, Ann laughed and told him his father would never allow him to take such filth into court. She was right. It was interesting, because when discussing the matter, Mr. Hopkins told David that, under the circumstances, he wouldn't object to the son killing the wife, then keeping his mouth shut, but certainly David couldn't divorce her and supply the press with that kind of manure.

"It was at this point that David's detective had an inspiration; an unfortunate one, because if it had never come about, David might still be alive. However, the detective had an idea: he searched out the Cutler homestead in West Virginia—or was it Kentucky?—and interviewed relatives who had never heard from her after she'd gone to New York, had never known her in her grand incarnation as Mrs. David Hopkins but simply as Mrs. Billy Joe Barnes, the wife of a hillbilly jarhead. The detective got a copy of the marriage certificate from the local courthouse, and after that he tracked down this Billy Joe Barnes, found him working as an airplane mechanic in San Diego, and persuaded him to sign an affidavit saying he had married one Ann Cutler, never divorced her, not remarried, that he simply had returned from Okinawa to find she had disappeared, but as far as he knew she was still Mrs. Billy Joe Barnes. Indeed she was!—even the cleverest criminal minds have a basic stupidity. And when David presented her with the information and said to her: 'Now we'll have no more of those round-figure ultimatums, since we're not legally married,' surely it was then she decided to kill him: a decision made by her genes, the inescapable white-trash slut inside her, even though she knew the Hopkinses would arrange a respectable 'divorce' and provide a very good allowance; but she also knew if she murdered David, and got away with it, she and her children would eventually receive his inheritance, something that wouldn't happen if he married Mary Kendall and had a second family.

"So she pretended to acquiesce and told David there was no point arguing as he obviously had her by the snatch, but would he continue to live with her for a month while she settled her affairs? He agreed, idiot; and immediately she began preparing the legend of the prowler—twice she called police, claiming a prowler was on the grounds; soon she had the servants and most of the neighbors convinced that prowlers were everywhere in the vicinity, and actually, Nini Wolcott's house was broken into, presumably by a burglar, but now even Nini admits that Ann must have done it. As you may recall, if you followed the case, the Hopkinses went to a party at the Wolcott's the night it happened. A Labor Day dinner dance with about fifty guests; I was there, and I sat next to David at dinner. He seemed very relaxed, full of smiles, I suppose because he thought he'd soon be rid of the bitch and married to his cousin Mary; but Ann was wearing a pale green dress, and she seemed almost green with tension— she chattered on like a lunatic chimpanzee about prowlers and burglars and how she always slept now with a shotgun by her bedside. According to the *Times*, David and Ann left the Wolcotts' a bit after midnight, and when they reached home, where the servants were on holiday and the children staying with their grandparents in Bar Harbor, they retired to separate bedrooms.

Ann's story was, and is, that she went straight to sleep but was wakened within half an hour by the noise of her bedroom door opening: she saw a shadowy figure—the prowler! She grabbed her shotgun and in the dark fired away, emptying both barrels. Then she turned on the lights and, oh, horror of horrors, discovered David sprawled in the hallway nicely cooled. But that isn't where the cops found him. Because that isn't where or how he was killed. The police found the body inside a glassed-in shower, naked. The water was still running, and the shower door was shattered with bullets."

In other words—" I began.

"In other words"—Lady Ina picked up but waited until a captain, supervised by a perspiring M. Soulé, had finished ladling out the soufflé Furstenberg—"none of Ann's story was true. God knows what she expected people to believe; but she just, after they reached home and David had stripped to take a shower, followed him there with a gun and shot him through the shower door. Perhaps she intended to say the prowler had stolen her shotgun and killed him. In that case, why didn't she call a doctor, call the police? Instead, she telephoned her *lawyer*. Yes. And *he* called the police. But not until *after* he had called the Hopkinses in Bar Harbor."

The priest was swilling another Gibson; Ann Hopkins, head bent, was still whispering at him confessionally. Her waxy fingers, unpainted and unadorned except for a stark gold wedding band, nibbled at her breast as though she were reading rosary beads.

"But if the police *knew* the truth—"

"Of course they knew."

"Then I don't see how she got away with it. It's not conceivable."

"I told you," Ina said tartly, "she got away with it because Hilda Hopkins wanted her to. It was the children: tragic enough to have lost their father, what purpose could it serve to see the mother convicted of murder? Hilda Hopkins, and old Mr. Hopkins, too, wanted Ann to go scot-free; and the Hopkinses, within their terrain, have the power to brainwash cops, reweave minds, move corpses from shower stalls to hallways; the power to control inquests—David's death was declared an accident at an inquest that lasted less than a day." She looked across at Ann Hopkins and her companion—the latter, his clerical brow scarlet with a two-cocktail flush, not listening now to the imploring murmur of his patroness but staring rather glassy-gaga at Mrs. Kennedy, as if any moment he might run amok and ask her to autograph a menu. "Hilda's behavior has been extraordinary. Flawless. One would never suspect she wasn't truly the affectionate, grieving protector of a bereaved and very legitimate widow. She never gives a dinner party without inviting her. The one thing I wonder is what everyone wonders—when they're alone, just the two of them, what do they talk about?" Ina selected from her salad a leaf of Bibb lettuce, pinned it to a fork, studied it through her black spectacles. "There is at least one respect in which the rich, the really very rich, *are* different from . . . other people. They understand *vegeta-*

bles. Other people—well, anyone can manage roast beef, a great steak, lobsters. But have you ever noticed how, in the homes of the very rich, at the Wrightsmans' or Dillons', at Bunny's and Babe's, they always serve only the most beautiful vegetables, and the greatest variety? The greenest *petits pois,* infinitesimal carrots, corn so baby-kerneled and tender it seems almost unborn, lima beans tinier than mice eyes, and the young asparagus! the limestone lettuce! the raw red mushrooms! zucchini . . ." Lady Ina was feeling her champagne.

Mrs. Matthau and Mrs. Cooper lingered over *café filtre.* "I know," mused Mrs. Matthau, who was analyzing the wife of a midnight-TV clown/hero, "Jane *is* pushy: all those telephone calls—Christ, she could dial Answer Prayer and talk an hour. But she's bright, she's fast on the draw, and when you think what she has to put up with. This last episode she told me about: hairraising. Well, Bobby had a week off from the show—he was so exhausted he told Jane he wanted just to stay home, spend the whole week slopping around in his pajamas, and Jane was ecstatic; she bought hundreds of magazines and books and new LP's and every kind of goody from Maison Glass. Oh, it was going to be a lovely week. Just Jane and Bobby sleeping and screwing and having baked potatoes with caviar for breakfast. But after one day he evaporated. Didn't come home night or call. It wasn't the first time, Jesus be, but Jane was out of her mind. Still, she couldn't report it to the police; what a sensation that would be. Another day passed, and not a word. Jane hadn't slept for forty-eight hours. Around three in the morning the phone rang. Bobby. Smashed. She said: 'My God, Bobby, where are you?' He said he was in Miami, and she said, losing her temper now, how the fuck did you get in Miami, and he said, oh, he'd gone to the airport and taken a plane, and she said what the fuck for, and he said just because he felt like being alone. Jane said: 'And *are* you alone?' Bobby, you know what a sadist he is behind that huckleberry grin, said: 'No. There's someone lying right here. She'd like to speak to you.' And on comes this scared little giggling peroxide voice: 'Really, is this really Mrs. Baxter, hee hee? I thought Bobby was making a funny, hee hee. We just heard on the radio how it was snowing there in New York—I mean, you ought to be down here with us where it's ninety degrees!' Jane said, very chiseled: 'I'm afraid I'm much too ill to travel.' And peroxide, all fluttery distress: 'Oh, gee, I'm sorry to hear that. What's the matter, honey?' Jane said: 'I've got a double dose of syph and the old clap-clap, all courtesy of that great comic, my husband, Bobby Baxter—and if you don't want the same, I suggest you get the hell out of there.' And she hung up."

Mrs. Cooper was amused, though not very; puzzled, rather. "How can any woman tolerate that? I'd divorce him."

"Of course you would. But then, you've got the two things Jane hasn't."

"Ah?"

"One: dough. And two: identity."

. . .

Lady Ina was ordering another bottle of Cristal. "Why not?" she asked, defiantly replying to my concerned expression. "Easy up, Jonesy. You won't have to carry me piggyback. I just feel like it: shattering the day into golden pieces." Now, I thought, she's going to tell me what she wants, but doesn't want to tell me. But no, not yet. Instead: "Would you care to hear a truly vile story? Really vomitous? Then look to your left. That sow sitting next to Betsy Whitney."

She *was* somewhat porcine, a swollen muscular baby with a freckled Bahamas-burnt face and squinty-mean eyes; she looked as if she wore tweed brassieres and played a lot of golf.

"The governor's wife?"

"The governor's wife," said Ina, nodding as she gazed with melancholy contempt at the homely beast, legal spouse of a former New York governor. "Believe it or not, but one of the most attractive guys who ever filled a pair of trousers used to get a hard-on every time he looked at that bull dyke. Sidney Dillon—" the name, pronounced by Ina, was a caressing hiss.

To be sure. Sidney Dillon. Conglomateur, adviser to Presidents, an old flame of Kate McCloud's. I remember once picking up a copy of what was, after the Bible and *The Murder of Roger Ackroyd*, Kate's favorite book, Isak Dinesen's *Out of Africa*; from between the pages fell a Polaroid picture of a swimmer standing at water's edge, a wiry well-constructed man with a hairy chest and a twinkle-grinning tough-Jew face; his bathing trunks were rolled to his knees, one hand rested sexily on a hip, and with the other he was pumping a dark fat mouth-watering dick. On the reverse side a notation, made in Kate's boyish script, read: *Sidney. Lago di Garda. En route to Venice. June, 1962.*

"Dill and I have always told each other everything. He was my lover for two years when I was just out of college and working at *Harper's Bazaar*. The only thing he ever specifically asked me never to repeat was this business about the governor's wife; I'm a bitch to tell it, and maybe I wouldn't if it wasn't for all these blissful bubbles risin' in my noggin—" She lifted her champagne and peered at me through its sunny effervescence. "Gentlemen, the question is: why would an educated, dynamic, very rich and well-hung Jew go bonkers for a cretinous Protestant size forty who wears low-heeled shoes and lavender water? Especially when he's married to Cleo Dillon, to my mind the most beautiful creature alive, always excepting the Garbo of even ten years ago (incidentally, I saw her last night at the Gunthers', and I must say the whole setup has taken on a very weathered look, dry and drafty, like an abandoned temple, something lost in the jungles at Angkor Wat; but that's what happens when you spend most of a life loving only yourself, and that not very much).

"Dill's in his sixties now; he could still have any woman he wants, yet for years he yearned after yonder porco. I'm sure he never entirely understood this ultra-perversion, the reason for it; or if he did, he never would admit it, not even to an analyst—that's a thought! Dill at an analyst! Men like that can never be analyzed because they don't consider any other man their equal. But as for the governor's wife, it was simply that for Dill she was the living incorporation of everything denied him, forbidden to him as a Jew, no matter how beguiling and rich he might be: the Racquet Club, Le Jockey, the Links, White's—all those places he would never sit down to a table of backgammon, all those golf courses where he would never sink a putt—the Everglades and the Seminole, the Maidstone, and St. Paul's and St. Mark's et al., the saintly little New England schools his sons would never attend. Whether he confesses to it or not, that's why he wanted to fuck the governor's wife, revenge himself on that smug hog-bottom, make her sweat and squeal and call him daddy. He kept his distance, though, and never hinted at any interest in the lady, but waited for the moment when the stars were in their correct constellation. It came unplanned—one night he went to a dinner party at the Cowleses'; Cleo had gone to a wedding in Boston. The governor's wife was seated next to him at dinner; she, too, had come alone, the governor off campaigning somewhere. Dill joked, he dazzled; she sat there pig-eyed and indifferent, but she didn't seem surprised when he rubbed his leg against hers, and when he asked if he might see her home, she nodded, not with much enthusiasm but with a decisiveness that made him feel she was ready to accept whatever he proposed.

"At that time Dill and Cleo were living in Greenwich; they'd sold their town house on Riverview Terrace and had only a two-room pied-à-terre at the Pierre, just a living room and a bedroom. In the car, after they'd left the Cowleses', he suggested they stop by the Pierre for a nightcap: he wanted her opinion of his new Bonnard. She said she would be pleased to give her opinion; and why shouldn't the idiot have one? Wasn't her husband on the board of directors at the Modern? When she'd seen the painting, he offered her a drink, and she said she'd like a brandy; she sip-sipped it, sitting opposite him across a coffee table, nothing at all happening between them, except that suddenly she was very talkative—about the horse sales in Saratoga, and a hole-by-hole golf game she'd played with Doc Holden at Lyford Cay; she talked about how much money Joan Payson had won from her at bridge and how the dentist she'd used since she was a little girl had died and now she didn't know *what* to do with her teeth; oh, she jabbered on until it was almost two, and Dill kept looking at his watch, not only because he'd had a long day and was anxious but because he expected Cleo back on an early plane from Boston: she'd said she would see him at the Pierre before he left for the office. So eventually, while she was rattling on about root canals, he shut her up: 'Excuse me, my dear, but do you want to fuck or not?' There is something to be said for aristocrats, even the stupidest have had some kind of class bred into them; so she shrugged —'Well, yes, I suppose so'—as though a salesgirl had asked if she liked the look of a hat. Merely resigned, as it were, to that old familiar hard-sell Jewish effrontery.

"In the bedroom she asked him not to turn on the lights. She was quite firm about that—and in view of what finally transpired, one can scarcely blame her. They undressed in the dark, and she took forever—unsnapping, untying, unzipping—and said not a word except to remark on the fact that the Dillons obviously slept in the same bed, since there was only the one; and he told her yes, he was affectionate, a mama's boy who couldn't sleep unless he had something soft to cuddle against. The governor's wife was neither a cuddler nor a kisser. Kissing her, according to Dill, was like playing post office with a dead and rotting whale: she really did need a dentist. None of his tricks caught her fancy, she just lay there, inert, like a missionary being outraged by a succession of sweating Swahilis. Dill couldn't come. He felt as though he were sloshing around in some strange puddle, the whole ambience so slippery he couldn't get a proper grip. He thought maybe if he went down on her—but the moment he started to, she hauled him up by his hair: 'Nononono, for God's sake, don't do that!' Dill gave up, he rolled over, he said: 'I don't suppose you'd blow me?' She didn't bother to reply, so he said okay, all right, just jack me off and we'll call it scratch, okay? But she was already up, and she asked him please not to turn on the light, please, and she said no, he need not see her home, stay where he was, go to sleep, and while he lay there listening to her dress he reached down to finger himself, and it felt . . . it felt . . . He jumped up and snapped on the light. His whole paraphernalia had felt sticky and strange. As though it were covered with blood. As it was. So was the bed. The sheets bloodied with stains the size of Brazil. The governor's wife had just picked up her purse, had just opened the door, and Dill said: 'What the hell is this? Why did you do it?' Then he knew why, not because she told him, but because of the glance he caught as she closed the door: like Carino, the cruel maître d' at the old Elmer's—leading some blue-suit brown-shoes hunker to a table in Siberia. She had mocked him, punished him for his Jewish presumption.

"Jonesy, you're not eating?"

"It isn't doing much for my appetite. This conversation."

"I warned you it was a vile story. And we haven't come to the best part yet."

"All right. I'm ready."

"No, Jonesy. Not if it's going to make you sick."

"I'll take my chances," I said.

Mrs. Kennedy and her sister had left; the governor's wife was leaving, Soulé beaming and bobbing in her wide-hipped wake. Mrs. Matthau and Mrs. Cooper were still present but silent, their ears perked to our conversation; Mrs. Matthau was kneading a fallen yellow rose petal—her fingers stiffened as Ina resumed: "Poor Dill didn't realize the extent of his difficulties until he'd stripped the sheets off the bed and found there were no clean ones to replace them. Cleo, you see, used the Pierre's linen and kept none of her own at the hotel. It was three o'clock in the morning and he couldn't reasonably call for maid service: what would he say, how could he explain the loss of his sheets at that hour? The particular hell of it was that Cleo would be sailing in from Boston in a matter of hours, and regardless of how much Dill screwed around, he'd always been scrupulous about never giving Cleo a clue; he really loved her, and, my God, what could he say when she saw the bed? He took a cold shower and tried to think of some buddy he could call and ask to hustle over with a change of sheets. There was me, of course; he trusted *me*, but I was in London. And there was his old valet, Wardell. Wardell was queer for Dill and had been a slave for twenty years just for the privilege of soaping him whenever Dill took his bath; but Wardell was old and arthritic, Dill *couldn't* call him in Greenwich and ask him to drive all the way in to town. Then it struck him that he had a hundred chums but really no friends, not the kind you ring at three in the morning. In his own company he employed more than six thousand people, but there was not one who had ever called him anything except *Mr. Dillon.* I mean, the guy was feeling sorry for himself. So he poured a truly stiff Scotch and started searching in the kitchen for a box of laundry soap, but he couldn't find any, and in the end had to use a bar of Guerlain's *Fleurs des Alpes.* To wash the sheets. He soaked them in the tub in scalding water. Scrubbed and scrubbed. Rinsed and scrubadubdubbed. There he was, the powerful Mr. Dillon, down on his knees and flogging away like a Spanish peasant at the side of a stream.

"It was five o'clock, it was six, the sweat poured off him, he felt as if he were trapped in a sauna; he said the next day when he weighed himself he'd lost eleven pounds. Full daylight was upon him before the sheets looked credibly white. But wet. He wondered if hanging them out the window might help—or merely attract the police? At last he thought of drying them in the kitchen oven. It was only one of those little hotel stoves, but he stuffed them in and set them to bake at four hundred fifty degrees. And they baked, brother: smoked and steamed—the bastard burned his hand pulling them out. Now it was eight o'clock and there was no time left. So he decided there was nothing to do but make up the bed with the steamy soggy sheets, climb between them and say his prayers. He really *was* praying when he started to snore. When he woke up it was noon, and there was a note on the bureau from Cleo: 'Darling, you were sleeping so soundly and sweetly that I just tiptoed in and changed and have gone on to Greenwich. Hurry home.' "

The Mesdames Cooper and Matthau, having heard their fill, self-consciously prepared to depart.

Mrs. Cooper said: "D-darling, there's the most m-m-marvelous auction at Parke Bernet this afternoon—Gothic tapestries."

"What the fuck," asked Mrs. Matthau, "would I do with a Gothic tapestry?"

Mrs. Cooper replied: "I thought they might be amusing for picnics at the beach. You know, spread them on the sands."

Lady Ina, after extracting from her purse a Bulgari vanity case made of white enamel sprinkled with diamond flakes, an object remindful of snow prisms, was dusting her face with a powder puff. She started with her chin, moved to her nose, and the next thing I knew she was slapping away at the lenses of her dark glasses.

And I said: "What are you doing, Ina?"

She said: "Damn! damn!" and pulled off the glasses and mopped them with a napkin. A tear had slid down to dangle like sweat at the tip of a nostril—not a pretty sight; neither were her eyes—red and veined from a heap of sleepless weeping. "I'm on my way to Mexico to get a divorce."

One wouldn't have thought that would make her unhappy; her husband was the stateliest bore in England, an ambitious achievement, considering some of the competition: the Earl of Derby, the Duke of Marlborough, to name but two. Certainly that was Lady Ina's opinion; still, I could understand why she married him—he was rich, he was technically alive, he was a "good gun" and for that reason reigned in hunting circles, boredom's Valhalla. Whereas Ina . . . Ina was fortyish and a multiple divorcée on the rebound from an affair with a Rothschild who had been satisfied with her as a mistress but hadn't thought her grand enough to wed. So Ina's friends were relieved when she returned from a shoot in Scotland engaged to Lord Coolbirth; true, the man was humorless, dull, sour as port decanted too long—but, all said and done, a lucrative catch.

"I know what you're thinking," Ina remarked, amid more tearful trickling. "That if I'm getting a good settlement, I ought to be congratulated. I don't deny Cool was tough to take. Like living with a suit of armor. But I did . . . feel safe. For the first time I felt I had a man I couldn't possibly lose. Who else would want him? But I've now learned this, Jonesy, and hark me well: there's always someone around to pick up an old husband. *Always.*" A crescendo of hiccups interrupted her: M. Soulé, observing from a concealed distance, pursed his lips. "I was careless. Lazy. But I just couldn't bear any more of those wet Scottish weekends with the bullets whizzing round, so he started going alone, and after a while I began to notice that everywhere he went Elda Morris was sure to go—whether it was a grouse shoot in the Hebrides or a boar hunt in Yugoslavia. She even tagged along to Spain when Franco gave that huge hunting party last October. But I didn't make too much of it—Elda's a great gun, but she's also a hard-boiled fifty-year-old virgin; I *still* can't conceive of Cool wanting to get into those rusty knickers."

Her hand weaved toward the champagne glass, but without arriving at its destination, drooped and fell like a drunk suddenly sprawling flat on the street. "Two weeks ago," she began, her voice slowed, her Montana accent becoming more manifest, "as Cool and I were winging to New York, I realized that he was staring at me with a, hmnnn, *ser*pentine scowl. Ordinarily he looks like an egg. It was only nine in the morning; nevertheless, we were drinking that loathsome airplane champagne, and when we'd finished a bottle and I saw he was still looking at me in this . . . homicidal . . . way, I said: 'What's bugging you, Cool?' And *he* said: 'Nothing that a divorce from you wouldn't cure.' Imagine the wickedness of it! springing something like that on a plane!—when you're stuck together for hours, and can't get away, can't shout or scream. It was doubly nasty of him because he knows I'm terrified of flying—he *knew* I was full of pills and booze. So now I'm on my way to Mexico." At last her hand retrieved the glass of Cristal; she sighed, a sound despondent as spiraling autumn leaves. "My kind of woman needs a man. Not for sex. Oh, I like a good screw. But I've had my share; I can do without it. But I can't live without a man. Women like me have no other focus, no other way of scheduling our lives; even if we hate him, even if he's an iron head with a cotton heart, it's better than this footloose routine. Freedom may be the most important thing in life, but there's such a thing as too much freedom. And I'm the wrong age now, I can't face all that again, the long hunt, the sitting up all night at Elmer's or Annabel's with some fat greaser swimming in a sea of stingers. All the old gal pals asking you to their little black-tie dinners and not really wanting an extra woman and wondering where they're going to find a 'suitable' extra man for an aging broad like Ina Coolbirth. As though there *were* any suitable extra men in New York. *Or* London. Or Butte, Montana, if it comes to that. They're all queer. Or *ought* to be. That's what I meant when I told Princess Margaret it was too bad she didn't like fags because it meant she would have a very lonely old age. Fags are the only people who are kind to worldly old women; and I adore them, I always have, but I really am not *ready* to become a full-time fag's moll; I'd rather go dyke.

"No, Jonesy, that's never been part of my repertoire, but I can see the appeal for a woman my age, someone who can't abide loneliness, who needs comfort and admiration: some dykes can ladle it out good. There's nothing cozier or safer than a nice little lez-nest. I remember when I saw Anita Hohnsbeen in Santa Fe. How I envied her. But I've always envied Anita. She was a senior at Sarah Lawrence when I was a freshman. I think everyone had a crush on Anita. She wasn't beautiful, even pretty, but she was so bright and nerveless and *clean*—her hair, her skin, she always looked like the first morning on earth. If she hadn't had all that glue, and if that climbing Southern mother of hers had stopped pushing her, I think she would have married an archaeologist and spent a happy lifetime excavating urns in Anatolia. But why disinter Anita's wretched history?—five husbands and one re-tarded child, just a waste until she'd had several hundred break-downs and weighed ninety pounds and her doctor sent her out to Santa Fe. Did you know Santa Fe is the dyke capital of the United States? What San Francisco is to *les garçons*, Santa Fe is to the Daughters of Bilitis. I suppose it's because the butchier ones like dragging up in boots and denim. There's a delicious woman there, Megan O'Meaghan, and Anita met her and, baby, that was *it*. All she'd ever needed was a good pair of motherly tits to suckle. Now she and Megan live in a rambling adobe in the foothills, and Anita looks . . . almost as clear-eyed as she did when we were at school together. Oh, it's a bit corny—the piñon fires, the Indian fetish dolls, Indian rugs, and the two ladies fussing in the kitchen over homemade tacos and the 'perfect' Margarita. But say what you will, it's one of the pleasantest homes I've ever been in. Lucky Anita!"

She lurched upward, a dolphin shattering the surface of the sea, pushed back the table (overturning a champagne glass), seized her purse, said: "Be right back"; and careened toward the mirrored door of the Côte Basque powder room.

Although the priest and the assassin were still whispering and sipping at their table, the restaurant's rooms had emptied, M. Soulé had retired. Only the hatcheck girl and a few waiters impatiently flicking napkins remained. Stewards were resetting the tables, sprucing the flowers for the evening visitors. It was an atmosphere of luxurious exhaustion, like a ripened, shedding rose, while all that waited outside was the failing New York afternoon.

TRUMAN CAPOTE was a native of New Orleans, where he was born on September 30, 1924. His first novel, *Other Voices, Other Rooms,* was an international literary success when first published in 1948, and accorded the author a prominent place among the writers of America's postwar generation. He sustained this position subsequently with short-story collections (*A Tree of Night,* among others); novels and novellas (*The Grass Harp* and *Breakfast at Tiffany's*); some of the best travel writing of our time (*Local Color*); profiles and reportage that appeared originally in *The New Yorker* (*The Duke in His Domain* and *The Muses Are Heard*); a true-crime masterpiece (*In Cold Blood*); several short memoirs about his childhood in the South (*A Christmas Memory, The Thanksgiving Visitor* and *One Christmas*); two plays (*The Grass Harp* and *House of Flowers*); and two films (*Beat the Devil* and *The Innocents*).

Mr. Capote twice won the O. Henry Memorial Short Story Prize and was a member of the National Institute of Arts and Letters. He died in August 1984, shortly before his sixtieth birthday.